THE WARRIOR

and

THE PETULANT PRINCESS

Maggie Carpenter

ADULT ADVISORY

This book is for adults only, and contains scenes of spanking, graphic sex, bondage, sensory deprivation, and are fantasies only, intended for adults. This book is not for children, nor does it condone corporal punishment of children. This book contains scenes of nonconsensual activities, BDSM and other nonconsensual activities. This book does not support nonconsensual spanking or any other nonconsensual activities, sexual or otherwise.

This book is a work of fiction. The characters, incidents, and dialogue are drawn from the author's imagination and are not to be construed as real. Any resemblance to actual events or persons, living or dead is entirely coincidental.

Published by Dark Secrets Press

DARK SECRETS PRESS

ISBN: 978-0692349182

Cover Design: Ashley@ Redbird Designs
Formatting: Polgarus Studio

Visit the author at:
www.Amazon.com/author/maggiecarpenter
www.maggiecarpenter.com
www.MaggieCarpenter.com/blog
www.facebook.com/MaggieCarpenterWriter
www.twitter.com/magcarpenter2

CONTENTS

CHAPTER ONE

O nce upon a time in a lustrous kingdom named Verdana, set amongst high-peaked mountains that glowed pink and gold when the two suns set, lived a strong-willed, petulant Princess named Lizbett, the only child of the kingdom's sovereign monarch, King Handerah.

From the time of her birth Lizbett had been headstrong and difficult. Blessed with both beauty and brains she had learned at an early age how to twist her doting father around her finger, and outsmart those who had been given the unenviable task of watching over her.

Her mother, Nydal, as wife of the Monarch, was the Kingdom's Ambassador and traveled a great deal. It was tradition that she fill this role, but when Lizbett took the throne her husband would be required to stay at her side, and an Ambassador would be assigned.

Whenever Nydal was home she too found Lizbett challenging. The ultimate result was predictable; Princess Lizbett grew to be fiercely independent, and she did as she pleased.

As she matured her beauty became legendary; sons from noble families and wealthy businessmen vied for her hand, and her father would encourage her, cajole her, even scold her, in an effort to convince her to say yes to one of them, but she would raise her eyebrows and state very simply "Oh, Father, they're all so boring," and with a flip of her very long, very curly, very red hair, that would be the end of it.

Much to his dismay he'd also received reports that Lizbett was discourteous to her adoring young men, and worse, gossip was beginning to spread through the Kingdom; Lizbett may be beautiful and possess high spirits, but she is less than agreeable to her eager suitors. The King did not like gossip, especially negative gossip about his daughter.

It was of great concern to Handerah. Not only was Lizbett at an age that she needed to find a suitable husband, she also had to carry the good name of the royal family into the future. She would have to raise her children, the future heirs to the monarchy, with the appropriate social skills and graces. He simply couldn't understand why she was so willful, and why she gave none of the eligible admirers the time of day.

The reason behind Lizbett's indifference was simple; her heart was already spoken for. Years earlier, when Lizbett was blossoming into womanhood, she had fallen madly in crush with a stable boy who had worked at the castle's stables for the summer.

She had been enchanted by him from the first moment he had handed her the reins of her horse. It was an especially warm season; the double suns would cross low the sky, and the days were long and hot.

His name was Larian; his hair fell in long shimmering ringlets around his head, and his clear aqua eyes would sparkle into hers. In spite of his youth he was tall with alarmingly wide shoulders, and she would lean her head against his chest, listening to the beating of his heart as his fingers trailed down her back, making her shiver with a hungry need.

"You are so spoiled," he would whisper. "When I am grown, and my life is my own, and I am practiced in the ways that will make me worthy of you, I will be back. Then I will teach you, I will teach you many things."

She would laugh and giggle, then with her violet eyes wide and her hunger surging between her legs, she would beg him to show her the ways of a man and woman.

"No, you must wait. You're too young, you're not ready," he'd whisper. "I have already been taught certain things, and I know that you have the craving of a woman, but you are still a child, and in many ways I am too."

But he would kiss her and fondle her breasts, and when she would pout and stamp her feet in protest because he refused to do more, he would sternly scold her.

"I have told you, no. You are used to getting your way but you will not with me, Princess, it will not happen, not yet."

"When?" she demanded.

"When I return," he promised.

"You're leaving? When? Where can you possibly go? You're just a stable boy."

He looked at her longingly, then tilted his head.

"One day you will come down here and find me gone, but you must not fret and you must be patient. I promise I will return."

When that sad day happened, it was when the warmth of the suns was waning, and cold nights had begun to spill across the kingdom. At the usual time she had run down to the stables for a kiss and a cuddle, aching to feel her heart thrill, and enjoy the hot wetness that would suddenly drool between her legs, but he was gone. The stable master, Tholl, a man who was big and burly and knew his place, politely informed her the lad had been collected early that morning and would not be back.

"Picked up by who?" she demanded. "You must tell me."

"I'm truly sorry, Princess, but I don't know," he replied, then frowning a frown she did not understand he lumbered away.

He did know, but had been sworn to secrecy the day the youth had first arrived, and again when he'd been collected.

She'd cried for days, then weeks, but the winter had set in, and there were balls and parties and dinners, visiting dignitaries and guests, and so she was distracted, but alone in her chamber when the darkness crept in, and the pink-silver twin moons would transit across her window, she would see his long locks and aqua eyes, and she would wonder what strange magic he had woven around her heart that she could not rid herself of him.

"You said you would return. When? Where did you go?" she would whisper, then slipping into sleep she would dream of him, and recall the shivers that would ripple through her from his touch.

The moons and suns crossed the skies many times, and the seasons came and went with annoying predictability, but still he lurked in the dark secret corridors of her mind, and when something reminded her of how her heart would beat as he held her, she would bristle with anger. How dare he promise to return and not do so?

Then the other feelings, the ones that made her skin tingle and pop into goosebumps, would surely wake from their sleep and leave her sad and restless.

One morning in early spring she decided to take her horse, Scarlet, out for a ride. Much to her father's displeasure she insisted on riding like a man. Her stockinged calves would show quite plainly and the women of the court would gossip about it endlessly.

"Such a shameful thing to do, " they would mutter behind their hands, but Lizbett didn't care. She liked to ride that way, and so she would, regardless of what the old biddies said.

The two suns were still rising, but shining as she set out, and Scarlet was full of pep and vim. The winter had begun wet and dreary, then the short, cold, snowy days had set in, and rides had become much too sparse for Lizbett and her mare, but with the onset of the bright spring weather she had ridden her every day, and they were both in excellent spirits as they made their way down the dirt road toward the fields. Not too far away was a waterfall that enchanted her; she'd not seen it since the previous summer, and with the spring thaws she was sure it would be cascading down the hill in breathtaking beauty.

She was trotting towards the bridge that would take her to the right trail, when she spied someone riding towards her. Rarely did she run across a stranger on the castle grounds, and whoever it was caught her attention, but not because she was surprised to see a stranger, but because he appeared to be a very impressive man on a very impressive horse.

He was mounted on a remarkable looking steed, big and black, with four white socks and a stunning white blaze splashed across his face. The horse was walking along quietly, unlike Scarlet who was jigging and tossing her head, behaving like the spirited, naughty mare that she was. As they drew closer Lizbett could see the man was dressed in fine attire that literally glinted, but with the East sun in her eyes she couldn't make out his features.

The narrow wooden bridge was approaching, and with room for only one to cross, realizing the stranger would reach his side first, Lizbett gave Scarlet a quick kick, and the mare, delighted at the prospect of a heartier pace bolted forward. To Lizbett's dismay they were just a few seconds too late, and arrived at the foot of the bridge at the same time the man began to cross; Lizbett had no choice but to pull the mare to an abrupt halt.

"Please, come forward, my lady," the stranger gallantly called as he backed up his horse.

"If you were going to let me pass, why did you enter the bridge in the first place?" she called back.

"You were traveling much too fast," he replied with the hint of a scolding tone. "It would not have been safe."

A sudden pulsing raced through her heart; his voice!

It couldn't be. No, Larian? No!

"I am not a child, Sir," she said tersely, ignoring the thumping in her chest, not wanting to believe it could be him but desperately hoping it was.

"Perhaps not in passes of the moons," he wryly remarked. "Are you coming across this bridge, my lady, or not?"

During the short exchange Scarlet had become increasingly agitated and was bouncing up and down, eager to move forward.

Not wanting to push her luck with the feisty mare Lizbett loosened her hold on the reins, freeing up the mare to jig forward, but she was holding her breath; in a matter of seconds she would know if it was Larian, or just a stranger whose voice had a similar tone.

Afraid to look she kept her eyes down as the mare carried her across, but once safely on the other side she took a deep breath and slowly lifted her eyes; her heart stopped thumping because it stopped completely.

"Larian," she whispered.

He had grown into a handsome, muscled man, the long golden ringlets had been trimmed close to his head, and his aqua eyes bored into hers as he stared at her.

"Good morning, Lizbett," he smiled, "it appears I didn't address you correctly."

"Excuse me?" she frowned turning Scarlet in a circle because she refused to stand still.

"I referred to you as, my lady, but I can see that title doesn't truly apply. The rumors I've heard are true."

Emotions swirling, Lizbett glared back at him.

"How dare you? You...you...disappear for years, then we meet and the first thing you do is insult me?" she huffed, "I am indeed a lady, and you are no gentleman to suggest otherwise."

"I am delighted to see you, Lizbett, of course I am, but saddened that it's obvious you have lacked the proper guidance, perhaps the appropriate discipline."

"I don't know what you're talking about," she blustered.

"Ladies do not have their legs over a horse in such a manner, they possess far more modesty. I can see almost to your knee, and the gossip I've heard about the way you've treated the young men who call on you! Really, Lizbett, shame on you."

He spoke with a quiet confidence that was unnerving, and at a complete loss she tossed her head in her usual manner and summoned her spirit.

"You're not my keeper, Larian, and you vanished without a word so you have no say about me, or about my life, or anything! It is I who has the right to ask the questions. You are, uh, you were just a stable boy. How have you risen so high in your life?"

"No, I am not your keeper," he frowned ignoring her inquiry, "but if I were responsible for you, you'd have far more in the way of manners; I have yet to hear you say thank you. I stopped you from a dangerous run across the bridge, then backed up my horse so you could move over it first."

"Thank you? You want me to thank you?" she exclaimed. "Not that I owe you an explanation, but the shock upon seeing you made me almost fall off. Should I thank you for that as well? Could you not have sent word?"

"My wish was to surprise you at the castle. I had no expectation of running into you on my ride there. I was just as surprised as you."

During the entire exchange Scarlet had been moving about, pawing at the ground and circling with agitation, while the big black horse had stood calmly still, content and happy.

"Hmmm," Larian mumbled eyeing her fidgety mare, "it appears you're not the only who could benefit from some training."

"You are insufferable!" she spat wishing she could bring herself to leave. "You weren't like this when I knew you before. You were kind, and sweet, and-"

"Where are you headed?" he interrupted.

"What business is it of yours?" she snapped.

"Lizbett, you must not be so quick to anger," he said softly. "Perhaps we should start over. Wherever you're headed I can accompany you. We can catch up. We should not begin our reunion this way."

She paused, staring at the boy who had become a man. He had once made her skin tingle and her stomach do a strange flippity flip, and she had adored him with her whole heart; suddenly it felt like only yesterday, and in that moment she knew it could happen again, the tingling, the happiness, the thrill; she knew it in the deepest part of her, and she wanted it.

"You're right, Larian," she purred, smiling so sweetly it would make the bees hum with joy, "I do thank you for allowing me to cross, and of course I would be so happy for you to join me. Please don't be angry with me."

Much to her astonishment he threw back his head and laughed out loud.

"What's so funny?" she asked trying to control her annoyance.

Rather than answer he continued to laugh, finally managing to compose himself.

"Lizbett, my dearest, Lizbett. Do not worry yourself, I'm not angry with you at all."

"Oh, good," she muttered a little unsure of herself.

"You are not to blame."

"Blame for what?" she asked her irritation unexpectedly returning. "What are you talking about?"

"Where are you headed?" he repeated ignoring her question.

"To the waterfall." *Do you remember, Larian, taking me there and laying next to me in the nearby meadow?*

"Ah, the waterfall, yes," he nodded.

"That's where I'm headed, and if you want you can come," she said impudently, though she hadn't meant to. She had wanted to welcome him to join her, but the way he had laughed…

CHAPTER TWO

It wasn't a long ride to the waterfall, and feeling somewhat unnerved she remained quiet, hoping Larian would carry the conversation and talk about where he'd been and what he'd been doing during his long absence, but all he did was make the occasional comment on the lush beauty the new season had brought forth.

Scarlet couldn't stop prancing while Larian's mount walked or trotted, moving easily from one gait to the next, and she couldn't help but be jealous of his horse's good behavior.

As they crested a small hill the meadow and waterfall came into view; the water was abundant and brilliant as it flowed down the mountainside, and the meadow was dense and rich. Dismounting and allowing their horses to graze they began to walk towards some weeping willows, a place they had often frequented.

"It is dazzling," she sighed relieved to have reached their destination. "I think this is my favorite place in the whole kingdom."

"Yes, it is truly lovely here," Larian said softly.

She looked up at his face and saw the memory of their youth, their days spent laying in the thick carpet of grass, his lips on hers, making her feel things, wish for things.

"You're remembering the days we spent here," she said wistfully.

"How could I not?" he admitted. "I have heard you have turned down many proposals. Are your memories of us the reason why? Have you been waiting for me as I asked you to?"

It was such an unexpected and direct question it caught her off guard. She wanted to say, yes; she wanted to admit her adoration of him had not waned, not one bit; she wanted to tell him that none of the men had made her stomach do that flippity flip thing, but her pride refused the confession.

"I've turned them down because men are such bores and I'm smarter than all of you," she replied, an evasive answer to his solemn and sincere questions.

"Perhaps," he said slowly, "that is not the whole truth."

"It is the truth," she flashed at him.

"There's that quick, nasty tongue," he remarked raising one scolding eyebrow. "Whether it be me or another, you need a man who will help you control that naughty temper and keep you happy and fulfilled, but in a manner that constantly reminds you of your place."

"My place? Larian, you forget I'm a Princess who will one day be Queen. I don't have a place, and even if I did no such man exists," she answered testily. "Take you, for instance," she said looking up at him, challenge her in violet eyes. "You took advantage of an innocent girl, then left her, promising to return, but you didn't, you didn't even write."

"But I have returned," he smiled. "Am I not here?"

"A bit late if you ask me," she muttered.

"I thought we were going to start over, no more angry words."

"I'm given to mood swings," she declared, "and when a mood takes me I go with it, and that, Larian, is just the way I am."

"Is that so? I disagree. You simply refuse to control yourself and that is not acceptable, especially not for one who will rule a kingdom, and I must say again, the manner in which you ride your horse; it's not right. You lay claim to being a Princess, yet you set such a dreadful example. How is it you're able to get away with such brazen behavior? Surely your father must object."

"My father has nothing to say about it, and as I said earlier, I shall ride as I like," she snapped, then added, "This conversation is irritating to me. We shall speak of something else."

"Shall we indeed?" he said moving towards her. "You've decreed it have you?"

Something in the way he was approaching her, his raised eyebrow, the look in his clear aqua eyes, made her stomach do the strange flippity flip; the flippity flip she had missed so much; the flippity flip she would feel when he once languished his lips upon her neck, or hold her hand, or trace her lips with his fingertips before kissing her. Feigning a confidence she did not feel, she replied,

"I am a Princess, and will one day be a Queen, and as such I can dictate the conversation, and you, Larian, you will bow to my wishes."

"Lizbett, you may call yourself a Princess, and you may have been born a Princess, but you behave like a spoiled, recalcitrant, child. To own the title, Princess, you must behave like a Princess, have grace and charm, manners and-"

"I have all those things," she interrupted, angrily staring at him.

"And as a spoiled, recalcitrant child," he continued, ignoring her remark, "I feel bound to treat you as such. I cannot allow you to continue to behave in such an outrageous manner, it would be irresponsible. What I am about to do I must; I must for the Kingdom, but more than that I must for you."

"What are you babbling about now?" she demanded, and though she was feigning a brave front the flippity flip thing in her stomach was telling her something dramatic, and possibly unpleasant was about to happen.

"I promised you that I would return when I was practiced and worthy. That time has come, Lizbett, and though you deny it I see in your eyes the true reason you have rejected all those who came calling for your hand. You have been waiting for me; in your heart you knew I would return to you."

His voice was soft, but confident and firm, and with a swift move he grabbed her hand, yanking her towards him.

"No, you're wrong," she quivered, her heart beating against her chest as the threat of prideful tears stung her eyes. "Let me GO! How dare you, you've become a brute!"

"Stop it, Lizbett, we both know I speak the truth."

He began walking, pulling her with him, and though she twisted and turned her wrist she was no match for his tight grip.

"Where do you think you're taking me?" she shrilled.

"To that fallen tree trunk, and I told you to be quiet!"

The will behind his command overwhelmed her, and she felt a vague, unfamiliar fear that sent her flippity flip tumbling furiously around her stomach.

"Stop, Larian, please, you're…you're scaring me."

"You know I care for you, and any pain you're about to experience is for your benefit."

"Pain? What pain? Larian, stop, what are you-?" but he'd reached his destination, and before she was able to finish he sat down and jerked her across his knee.

"AAARGH! LARIAN!"

"Now, Princess, we shall see who dictates the conversation."

Holding her firmly he began bouncing his hand off her upturned bottom, eliciting loud squeals of shock.

"STOP! STOP!" she wailed. "HOW DARE YOU!"

"You have been needing this for a very long time," he exclaimed, his hand landing blow after blow. "I will not bare you completely, but I'm going to lift your dress in a minute so you'd better prepare yourself."

"No! Don't you dare! I shall have you thrown in a dungeon and-"

"Until I tell you otherwise you will address me as Sir," he interjected, pausing his hand to issue his decree, "and if you continue to protest I will absolutely expose your flesh, so please, keep up your kicking and screaming, I would love to see the results of my handiwork."

Though her face was burning with humiliation and anger, it turned an even deeper crimson at the suggestion, and while she was appalled and astonished she wasn't stupid; in her heart she knew him, and she had no doubt he would do as he threatened.

A moment later she felt it; he was lifting her dress. She wanted to cry out, to protest loudly and kick with all her might, but his threat rang in her ears; she wouldn't be able to stand it if he exposed her.

Slowly, deliberately, he moved layer after layer of petticoats over her back; he had been taught well and was no stranger to the deed. He was hoping that his agonizing pace would propel her into protestations so he could keep his promise and pull down her drawers, but it seemed she was as smart as she was beautiful and willful. Finally staring at her round contours, hidden only by the thinnest piece of silk, he rested his palm, relishing the sight and feel of her almost naked backside.

"Now, Lizbett, you shall feel the heat of my hand, and you shall take notice."

She was horrified that he was staring at her underwear, but at the first slap of his stinging hand her modesty fell away.

"OW! That hurt."

"Yes, Lizbett, it's supposed to hurt," he declared landing a second.

"OUCH! Sir, please!"

"Now Lizbett," he continued as his hand rose and fell, "you will no longer be rude, or ride your horse in that unladylike fashion, and you will listen to your father and do as he says."

"Yes, Sir, yes, I promise" she cried, wincing and crying out as each slap fell, "now would you, please, STOP!"

"The days that you issue commands are over," he admonished. "I shall spank you as you deserve, and if you dare to bark at me again I will keep my promise and remove this thin undergarment."

"NO! Please, Sir, no, I'll be good, I'm sorry!"

"Obedience! Finally! That's something new for you, isn't it Lizbett?"

"Yes, sir," she whimpered.

"I am going to finish what I've started and spank you as I see fit. If you truly don't want me to bare your bottom, I suggest you take your discipline without further argument. I will not warn you again. Do you understand?"

"Yes, Sir, I understand," she bleated.

Resuming his work he laid on slow solid swats, allowing the impact of each to register, and when he delivered a final volley dispatched with stinging speed, though she gasped and wriggled she did not protest.

"I'm done for a moment, Lizbett," he said, his voice suddenly tender as he smoothed his hand over the flimsy fabric. "I've made very clear what I expect from you. Is there anything you don't understand? It's quite simple, behave as a Princess should."

"I understand, Sir," she whimpered.

"Next time I see you riding you'll be in the proper saddle, correct?"

"Yes, Sir," she stammered.

"And if someone, anyone, is kind to you, extends a favor, what will you do?"

"Say thank you."

"Excellent. You see, you know exactly how to behave. Your lack of manners and grace is nothing more than conceit and attitude, isn't it, Lizbett?"

"Yes, Sir," she murmured as a fresh streak of humiliation washed through her.

"Good girl," he crooned as his hand continued to rub away the sting. "The first step in correcting your ways is admitting you know better."

Lizbett felt a warm, strange, wonderfulness, and she suddenly had a great need to curl herself into his lap.

"You may crawl off now. Lay at my feet and I will hold you as I used to."

As she slid off him on to the grass, her petticoats and dress falling around her, he dropped on the ground beside her and immediately wrapped her in his arms. The smell of her hair, the fit of her body against his, the press of her breasts against his chest, was familiar and warm and he felt gloriously complete.

"My bottom hurts," she whined.

"I know, my sweet Lizbett, as it should. Your bottom should be made hot on a regular basis. You need strong, loving discipline."

"I'll be good now," she vowed shifting back and lifting her eyes to meet his. "I will, I swear it."

"You feel that way now, but in a little while, a day, a week, you will be petulant and stubborn again, your temper will blaze, and then you will need to be reminded, and that reminder will be in the form of punishment."

"But I won't, honest."

"Oh, Lizbett, if only that were true," he sighed, "but we will not speak of this further. There is something else that needs attention."

"There is?"

"Yes, there, is," he purred, and moving his hand to the back of her head he clutched a fistful of her long, curly, red hair. "Close your eyes."

She could feel her heart pounding and the delicious hot wetness surging between her legs. His lips brushed against hers, and uttering a moan of hungry need she surrendered her mouth, sinking into his kiss. The flippity flip transformed into a thousand butterflies as her arms moved around his neck, urgently clinging, and when he finally pulled back she let out a choked cry.

"Larian, I have missed you so."

"Lizbett, such a heartfelt, honest confession. This is the real Lizbett and I am so happy to see you. I have missed you as well, very much. I could not write, I was far away, immersed in my education, but now that is over. Now I am here to speak to your father, about you and me, but only if you want me to."

"Oh, I do," she breathed.

"It will mean many spankings, Lizbett, all kinds of spankings."

"But I will be good, Larian, you won't have to spank me."

The comment sent a broad smile across his face and he kissed her lightly.

"I'll do other things as well, all sorts of things."

"Like what?"

"Tie you up, blindfold you, make you kneel in supplication before me."

A gentle shiver rattled down her spine as a fresh surge of sexual energy swept through her body, and her entire being began to tingle.

"Larian." she whispered, "I want you. Do what you will."

"Then we will ride back to the castle and I will speak with the King. He is expecting my visit."

"You wrote to him but not me?" she frowned.

"I told you, I wanted to surprise you."

"Oh, yes, that's right."

"Do I detect a little petulance from my Princess already?"

"No, no," she said quickly.

"Will you be able to ride?" he asked releasing her from his hug and sitting up.

"Um, yes, I think so, maybe a bit uncomfortably," she replied feeling oddly shy.

"I'm pleased that this will be the last time I'll be seeing you straddled in such an unseemly fashion," he remarked standing up and reaching for her hand.

"I do prefer riding the way men do," she sighed as she rose to her feet. "It's so much easier."

"Perhaps there is a compromise," he offered putting an arm around her and walking them back to their horses.

"There is?"

"In public, you will ride in a way that befits your station, as both a woman and a Princess, but when we are alone you will be permitted to ride as you like."

"Larian, that's an excellent suggestion. I approve."

"You approve?" he grinned down at her.

"I do," she declared.

Taking hold of Scarlet's reins he handed them over to her. *You have much to learn, Lizbett, and learn you shall.*

CHAPTER THREE

A s they approached the castle the guards in the turrets called for the drawbridge to be lowered. The moat's baby pink water that appeared so inviting was lethal should anyone attempt to swim across; the pink was created by an algae that stung any living creature, man or animal, to its death. Though the times were peaceful, the King had created that peace through strength, but in so doing had made some vengeful adversaries.

"There is nothing so inviting as a King who has not been beaten," he'd once told Lizbett. "Treat the populace fairly, be generous and merciful, and if the Kingdom is ever in jeopardy they will rise to your aid, not side with the enemy."

Handerah was in his court listening to gripes and offering advice to those fortunate enough to have been granted an audience. He opened his doors often, and regardless of their reason for wishing to be heard he would listen patiently, then treat the visitor to a sumptuous buffet after their consult.

But the King was no fool, and lurking in the crowd were trusted servants who listened to the conversations, determining if there was dissent and taking note of any praise. Handerah loved his Kingdom and its people, and he knew it was important to keep an ear to the ground so he could address any unrest quickly, whether by a strong hand or a generous one. The unknown spies in the crowd was only one of several covert methods he had in place to remain informed; his rule was stable and he intended to keep it that way.

Though Larian didn't know the details of Handerah's methods, he was aware of the King's strong but loving leadership, and how deeply he was respected and admired by the neighboring realms and noble families. Many had tried to emulate Handerah's style but he was unique; it wasn't just what he did, it was how he did it.

For Larian, however, Handerah was a puzzle.

How could a man so indomitable, have failed to raise his daughter with the same caring but unconquerable will? How was it that the beautiful Princess had ended up such a pampered, petulant brat?

As they entered the courtyard the stable hands rushed to help her, but as she slid off her saddle and petted her mare the young men hung back, their heads bowed.

"You may take her," she finally decreed.

Tholl had lumbered out to oversee things and recognized Larian immediately.

"Larian, look at you. What a man you've become," he exclaimed, "and what a steed you have."

"This is Thunder, because that's what he sounds like at a full gallop."

"I can well imagine," Tholl grinned. "Larian, I am so proud. I've heard tell of your many achievements."

"What achievements?" Lizbett interrupted. "Did you win some contests?"

"Thank you, Tholl, and it's marvelous to see how well you look," Larian replied ignoring Lizbett's inquiry.

"Thank you, may I take your horse? What a beauty he is."

"Yes, please, he's had a long journey. He needs water, as much hay as he wants and a soft bed," Larian said pulling a large cloth bag from the side of the saddle.

"He shall have it all," Tholl promised with a slight bow of his head.

"Larian," Lizbett interjected again. "By achievements does he mean contests? Did you win some contests?"

"No, Lizbett, not exactly," Larian patiently replied, and slinging the bag over his shoulder he placed his hand at the small of her back and guided her to the door that would take them inside the castle. "I might tell you what Tholl was referring to later."

"Might? What do you mean, might? I insist."

"I thought you said you were going to be a good girl," he remarked raising his one eyebrow.

"I will, I am, I'm just-"

"Being pushy and rude," he finished. "My audience with your father is in a short while and I'd like to freshen up. He's expecting me to stay at least a couple of days. Who should I speak with about my accommodation?"

"Oh, that would be Delina. She's in charge of our guests, but I'm surprised. Only important people stay here in the castle. My father invited you? For two days? I don't understand."

"I'll explain, but not right now," he said firmly. "Where can I find her?"

"She'll probably be in the receiving room."

As they walked through the wide, opulent passageway, everyone they passed lowered their eyes, and if they were in conversation they stopped speaking as Lizbett passed by. It seemed to Larian they were afraid of her, and he wasn't very pleased with the look in their eyes when their gaze dropped as she approached.

At the end of the hallway was a large, arched double door, and pushing it open Lizbett gestured for him to enter. An older but handsome woman was seated behind a large desk, and stood up and smiled as he moved towards her.

"You must be Larian," she smiled. "First, may I say what an honor this is. The King has spoken of little else since he received your letter, and The Queen was deeply disappointed that she is missing your visit. She was so looking forward to seeing you."

"Thank you, Delina. Yes, I would very much have enjoyed meeting with the Queen. She is a remarkable woman."

Lizbett listened to the exchange in complete bewilderment. Larian may have improved his station in life, but Delina was carrying on as if he was a noble, and to say her mother was sorry to have missed him was very strange. Her mother met with the royalty of other Kingdoms all the time, and did nothing but complain about the chore. Larian had been a mere stable boy when he'd been there in his youth; none of what she was hearing made any sense.

"Which is his chamber?" Lizbett asked sharply. "He's tired, he's been riding for…well…a long time. He needs to-"

"Lizbett," Larian said quietly, dropping his head and catching her eye, "I'm perfectly capable of speaking for myself."

Though unsure whether Delina had heard the discreet reprimand Lizbett felt a flush of embarrassment, and nervously ran her hand through her long, red hair.

"I will ring for the boy to show you the way," Delina smiled, and moving to a rope hanging from the wall she gave it a sharp tug. "There are refreshments waiting for you, Larian. Some billberry wine, some of our wonderful breads, and a few other foods you might find appetizing. Ah, here he is. Boy! Show our guest to Chamber Five."

Lizbett stared in wonder. Chamber Five was their finest guest apartment, and held in reserve for the most important of visiting dignitaries. Before she could comment the boy hurried forward, and with a strength that belied his size, threw the bag over his shoulder just as Larian had done, then stood waiting, staring at Larian for his cue to move.

"Thank you, Delina. Will I be seeing you later?"

"Yes, Larian, at the dinner the King has arranged to welcome you," she replied.

"That's very kind of him," Larian remarked. "Then I shall see you there. Boy, if you would, please show me to my chamber."

"Yes, Sir," the boy nodded.

Lizbett stared at Delina for some kind of clue, but she was already back at her desk with her head focused on some papers in front of her.

Father has arranged a dinner to welcome him? What is going on? I knew there was a banquet tonight, but for Larian? First I've heard of this.

Though Lizbett was anxious to speak, to ask a thousand-and-one questions, Larian's quiet scolding was keeping her tongue still, but she was determined to interrogate him the moment they were alone. As she caught up to him in the hallway he lowered his lips to her ear.

"You will come into the chamber with me and stay quietly. You will not speak until I ask you to. Understood?"

"What? Why?" she muttered.

"Understood has only two possible answers," he quipped, "neither of which I heard."

"But-"

"You have one more chance to answer correctly."

"Oh, uh, yes," she mumbled.

"Yes, what?"

"Uh, yes, Larian, I understand," she whispered.

A trembling warmth was flooding her sex, and as they moved up the few steps to the landing that would lead into Chamber Five, she felt a sudden weakness and leaned against the wall for support. Larian, with a knowing look in his eye, smiled down at her.

"Lizbett? Do you need help?"

"No, I'm fine, just a bit…uh…I'm fine," she stammered.

The boy had already entered the room and was placing the bag on the low trunk at the foot of the bed.

"If you're fine, then please go in ahead of me and sit down," he said softly. "I don't need you fainting, but the rule still applies. You will not speak until I give you permission."

"But why?" she mumbled.

She was rewarded with a smile and a shake of his head, and with a swift move of his hand he grabbed her elbow and began to shuffle her inside.

"I can manage," she said curtly, but when she attempted to pull her elbow from his grasp she found it impossible.

"Thank you, boy, that will be all."

The boy had been standing next to the bag with his eyes downcast, and with a quick nod he hurried out the door closing it behind him.

"Would you please let go of me and tell me who you are?" Lizbett demanded. "I mean, who you are really? Why were you working here as a stable hand if you're someone so important? I don't understand any of this."

Dropping her elbow Larian moved across to the door and checked that it was locked, then returning swiftly to his bag he withdrew what looked like a horse's bit, but it had thin leather straps on either end.

"You are a very naughty girl," Larian declared walking towards her. "I gave you a simple instruction and you not only chose to ignore it, you began questioning me as if I was one of your servants."

"I have a right to know about-"

"You will sit, immediately," he growled, "unless you want me to turn you over my knee again, and bare your bottom for more punishment."

"You wouldn't, not here, not in the castle," she gasped. "No, you wouldn't."

"If you don't sit down right now, you'll find out," he said sternly.

Quivering, Lizbett moved quickly to the chair by the desk near the fireplace and perched herself on the edge of the seat.

"Wise decision," he said solemnly. "Now, with no back talk, no arguments, no questions, close your eyes and open your mouth."

She stared at the odd bit-like object in his hand, a rush of fear shivering through her, but afraid he would indeed, throw her over his lap and bare her bottom, she did as he instructed.

It was a flash of seconds before the rubber bit was between her lips, and the leather straps were being buckled behind her head. She let out a muffled cry of protest, but the bit was effective and she couldn't form any words.

"There, now perhaps I can have a moment or two of peace, and you will learn another lesson. When I instruct you to be quiet and not speak until I give permission, I mean it. If you don't wish to obey me then you will face the consequence."

Lizbett stared up at him, her eyes wide in disbelief, and in a moment of rebellious fury she stamped her feet on the floor.

"If you do that again," he said quietly leaning over her and fixing her with steely glare, "I will tie your ankles to the chair, and when I eventually let you go I will strip you completely naked, and then spank you. It won't just be your bottom that will be open to my eye."

Her brow crinkled in dismay, and Larian raised his hand and ran his fingertips across her cheek.

"Princess, I adore you, but if you wish to be with me you will learn obedience. You must," he said firmly. "I intended to tell you everything about me when we came in here. I wanted to sit with you, eat with you, and drink with you, but you made that impossible. Lessons must come first, so instead of enjoying our reunion with wine, you will ponder your behavior with a bit in your mouth. Do you understand?"

Lizbett gazed up at him and slowly nodded her head.

"Good girl. Now, I must wash and change. You stay exactly where you are. Let's see if you're capable of controlling yourself long enough to do that."

CHAPTER FOUR

As he freshened up and changed his clothes in the anteroom off the bed chamber, he wondered if he'd find his naughty Princess still waiting for him when he returned. He had purposely left her hands and feet free; she could easily unbuckle the bit, and just as easily get up and leave. If she obeyed him all would be well, and though her education would be challenging it was a task he was eager to undertake, but if she bolted it would call into question his judgement, how he had assessed her and the feelings she held for him.

When he was near the end of his training and finally permitted to receive news from the outside, he'd not been at all surprised when he'd heard about the pampered, petulant Princess and her impossible behavior. Though she had been difficult in their youth he had recognized an inherent passion and spirit that was separate from her willful ways. The summer that he'd worked as a stable boy he had fallen utterly in love with her, and when he'd promised to return he'd meant it.

The suns and moons had crossed the sky many times during his rigorous schooling, and though theirs had been a young love, his feelings for her had not passed with time, and she had remained in his heart.

Even as the Vest of Accomplishment had been slid up his arms, and the ruler of his Principality had announced Larian had reached the rank of Warrior Of The First Order, a title bestowed upon only a few, the memory of her was alive. Later that night at the banquet to celebrate the achievement, the Prince had risen from his throne and called the banquet to silence.

"It is with great pride I state the following. Lord Larian Lobergene received the highest acclaim from the Captains of each of the skills and has earned the rank of Commander. With great honor he will have a residence and lands. He may stay within the realm, or travel the lands as he chooses to rest his body and mind from the rigors of his training."

As was the custom, the guests rose from their chairs while Larian remained seated, and lifting their goblets high in the air they called out his name. It was a solemn toast, the highest praise for a young man who had committed his energies to become a warrior for the realm, and as they took their seats, with humility and eyes lowered he left his chair and moved to kneel before his ruler.

"I thank you my Prince, and with your permission will leave for a short time, but only to pursue a maiden," he'd declared, his head bowed.

"Seek her, and we pray you will win her," the Prince had said in a rare moment of tenderness.

With his Ruler's blessing, the following day Larian had written to King Handerah to beg the monarch's permission to court his daughter.

The King's enthusiastic reply had filled his heart, and he'd set off on the long journey to return to the Kingdom where Tholl had so diligently and thoroughly taught him about horses and their care. The last thing Larian had expected was to cross paths with the recalcitrant Princess on his way through the castle grounds. Meeting her at the wooden narrow bridge had been a delightful surprise, and he'd taken it as a sign the Gods were smiling upon him. He'd not expected to have her over his knee so soon, but when it became obvious it had to be done he didn't hesitate, and what a joy it had been to bounce his hand of her well-deserving, beautiful bottom.

In the anteroom, staring at his reflection as he donned his clean white shirt and maroon vest embroidered with the finest gold and silver thread, a replica of The Vest Of Accomplishment, he broke into a wry grin as he recalled the picture of Lizbett's backside through her thin silk drawers just a short time before.

"What a truly naughty Princess you are," he muttered, "so much naughtier than I expected. Your bottom must be red and stinging frequently, and if you're still in that chair waiting for me I will see to it; make no mistake, Lizbett, I will see to it."

Taking a deep breath, knowing there was every possibility Lizbett's pride may have taken hold and she'd be gone, he pushed down the handle and cracked the door to peer into the room; his heart did a tiny leap; she had fought her demons and won.

"Thank you," he murmured, his gratitude being sent both to her, and the Gods.

Larian was right. She had fought her demons, and it had been a fierce battle. Her pride had risen up, urging her to rip off the bit, hurl it into the fireplace and march furiously from the room. Visions of banging on the door of the anteroom, yelling at him for being such a beast had danced in her head, and threats that she would have him thrown in a dungeon had flashed through her mind.

I am the daughter of the mighty King Handerah! Larian cannot treat me this way, he cannot! How dare he expect me to sit here and bend to his will. The foolish man has left me untied. Does he think I won't spit out this dreadful thing in my mouth and hurl it at him when he returns?

But each time she had been on the verge of raising her hands to unclasp the buckle behind her head, something had stopped her; when her feet had planted themselves firmly on the ground and she was about to rise, she didn't, and it wasn't just her raging curiosity about why he was being treated with such honor.

She wanted him.

She wanted his arms around her; his lips against hers; she wanted to lean against his chest and nestle into his body, and an unfamiliar desire rising up from her soul, wanted to please him. It was a strong desire, a heavy desire, and the fevered conflict had begun to abate; finally resigned she'd sunk into the chair.

"What a good girl," he announced as he reappeared, sending a surge of warmth through her heart. "I have just enough time to share a quick meal before I must make my way to court."

He was ambling towards her, a half-smile on his face, and an expression she couldn't read.

"I'm proud of you, Lizbett. I'm sure you were tempted to pull off your discipline bit and run out of here. If I remove it now, will you continue to be a good girl?"

She stared up at him, slowly nodding her head. An odd feeling of tears bristled just below the surface and she didn't know why. Lizbett didn't cry, not ever, not about anything.

You're making me feel things, strange things, things I didn't feel when we were together before. What are you doing to me? Are you a sorcerer? Are you casting a spell?

"I would much rather be kissing your mouth instead of punishing it, but if you insist on interrupting and speaking when you shouldn't then it must be so. If you do those things again, the bit returns. Understand?"

She nodded her head, and as her eyes gazed into his a wave of heavy emotion sent her flippity flips flipping.

Please take me in your arms, please stroke my back, please hold-

"Perhaps you have learned," he remarked breaking into her thoughts, and walking behind her he gently unbuckled the leather straps.

"Ooh, Larian, that was very difficult," she breathed, rubbing her jaw with her hands.

"It was supposed to be. Lessons are only learned if they are difficult. Give me your hand."

He reached out, and as he pulled her into his chest, and held her in a firm, gentle embrace, she dissolved against him.

"I could stay here forever," she whispered.

Closing his eyes he drank in the feel of her, and willed his surging cock to return to sleep.

"Come, we'll drink and eat a little before I leave," he murmured, indulging himself for just a moment to lean in and kiss her neck.

She moaned as his lips touched her skin, and she pressed against him, tilting her head to the side begging for more.

"Please, Larian, please won't you-?"

"No, my sweet Lizbett," he breathed. "Come with me now, I must eat."

Leading her to the table set against the paned windows, he pulled out her chair, then sat opposite, and lifted the thin cloth covering the meal laid out for him.

"This is so thoughtful," he sighed. "I am quite hungry. I've not eaten since the dawn of the East sun."

"Since the dawn of the East sun?" she gasped. "How can that be?"

"It is nothing," he replied taking some of the seeded bread and spreading it with cheese and nuts. "I have gone through several passes of the moons with nothing to eat, but that which I could find under the leaves on the forest floor, or hanging from the branches of trees."

"That sounds terrible," she frowned.

"It is terrible, but it is also a necessary lesson. It taught me to be grateful for the fine food that crosses my plate, and if I ever need to I can survive with nothing provided."

"Um, Larian, may I ask...?"

"Ah, manners," he smiled, pouring some purplish wine from a carafe. "How delightful to hear you ask in such a polite way. When you do I am obliged to answer."

Momentarily speechless she watched him raise the goblet to his lips; his compliment had sent a fresh ripple of delighted satisfaction through her heart; she had pleased him and it felt sublime.

"You are not from lowly birth as I thought," she said softly. "I am so puzzled by everything. Please, can you tell me something of who you really are?"

"Of course," he said. "This wine is excellent. Would you care for some?"

"I would, very much," she nodded.

"I believe either a please or thank you belongs on the end of that sentence," he remarked.

"Oh, yes, I would, very much, please," she blushed.

"I shall be watching you very carefully at dinner, Lizbett. I expect nothing but courtesy and humble manners."

"I'll do my best," she promised watching him pour the wine into her goblet. "Please will you tell me about your family, explain this mystery to me?"

"My name is Lord Larian Lobergene, and I am from the Principality of Zanderone. My cousin, Fenderon, is the ruler."

"Zanderone? You are a Lord from Zanderone? The men from Zanderone have fought beside the soldiers in my father's army. They are mighty warriors. I've heard they are skilled in many things, not just fighting battles. Is that why you said you were immersed in your education? Why you were eating from the forest floor?"

"It is, Lizbett, and it is why I was sent here for the summer as a youth and slept in your barn with the horses. One cannot be a true and accomplished horseman if one does not know how a horse thinks and feels."

"Oh, my goodness," she exclaimed. "I…uh…had no idea."

"Tholl taught me how to make their feet healthy and strong, how to find answers to their ills and treat them. Without our horses how would we do anything? When I returned home I spent one hundred passes of the moons living in our stables and caring for our mounts, then I was tested by the Captain Of The Steeds. Had I not passed I would have been sent back here to begin again."

"This is so much to take in."

"It was the same for each of the things I had to learn. I was sent to different places for the basics, then once home I was immersed in that particular area of education."

"Are you saying…are you a warrior?" she breathed stunned by the news.

"I am, Lizbett," he nodded.

"Now I understand why you didn't write," she murmured, "but why…uh…sorry…may I ask, why didn't you tell me you were from Zanderone, or that you were in training to become a warrior?"

"Only your father and mother knew, and Tholl of course, otherwise I would have been treated differently. I had to learn as a mere stable boy learns, and to be treated as such. It is humbling and it is necessary. You would benefit greatly from such an ordeal."

"I'm not sure I wish to sleep in a stable," she frowned, then pausing, her eyes locking his, she took a deep breath and whispered, "I had dreams of us running away from here. My father would never have allowed a marriage to a stable boy, but I wanted to be with you that much."

"That was evident," he said tenderly, "and it was one of the things that touched me so deeply."

"I'm not sure I understand?"

"You listened to your heart. You cared for a stable boy. It showed me that your heart is true. You may be a spoiled brat, but your heart, it shines."

Again she felt the brimming of unexpected tears, and dropping her eyes she reached for her goblet.

"It is unfortunate that you do not care what your father thinks," he sighed. "The way-"

"I do though," she interrupted, then quickly added, "sorry, I didn't mean to cut you off, but I do care, kind of, inside me."

His aqua eyes sparkled across at her.

"I was about to say, the way you ride, and the manner in which you treat others; every time you are rude or arrogant you show the world you do not care what your father thinks. He is a great King, you are his daughter, yet you do not emulate him or behave as he would like."

"I…uh…never thought about it like that," she muttered. "I do care, I just want to do things my way."

"It's time you began to grow up, Princess. Only a child insists on things being their way."

"I suppose…" she said, her voice trailing off.

"I must leave. That was a lovely meal, beautifully presented. Who would have arranged this?"

"Delina I would think, yes, Delina."

"Then I must stop by her office and thank her on my way back from seeing your father at court."

"I'm coming with you," she announced jumping from her seat.

Larian leaned back in his chair and fixed her with a scolding look.

"What? You don't want me to?"

"I do not want you to presume," he said slowly.

Lizbett felt a hot blush cross her face.

"I don't know what to say," she mumbled.

"You cannot come to court with me. My audience with your father is one I must take with him alone, but I will request that you be seated nearby at dinner."

"Nearby? But I want to be next to you, right next to you."

Larian rose from his chair, took her hand and led her to the door.

"It's time for you to leave, and as far as being seated next to me, that privilege, Princess, will have to be earned," and ushering her on to the landing, he turned and walked back inside.

Lizbett stared at the closed door, not quite sure what was happening. Things were upside-down. Larian was suddenly in control, and while there was a thrill attached to the experience, it was not the way she was used to living her life.

Sitting next to you will have to be earned? I didn't have to earn your kisses when we were younger. I certainly didn't have to earn that mighty spanking you gave me...or wait, did I? This is all so befuddling. You're here to talk to my father about us, that's what you said, but you won't sit next to me? This is nonsense. I'll will sit next to you, I'll make sure of it.

She began marching purposefully towards the hallway that would take her to the kitchen, then stopped, reconsidering what she was about to do.

If I order my place be next to his, then I'll only make him angry at me again because it's not what he wants. I don't want that. This is very difficult. Hmmm, it's just one dinner. I'll have a lifetime of dinners to sit next to him. Better I remain compliant, at least for now. Yes, that's what I must do, be compliant. I can do that.

Feeling very pleased with herself she returned to her apartment to select the dress she would wear for the banquet, determined she would be the most beautiful of them all, and make him sorry he was not beside her.

CHAPTER FIVE

King Handerah had scheduled Larian's audience to be the last of the day. He needed to spend some time with the young warrior and he certainly wouldn't have the opportunity at the banquet that evening.

Having finished with his last visitor he needed to gather his thoughts, and gestured to the page to wait before opening the door to allow Larian to enter, then rising from his dark wood, heavily carved throne he began to slowly pace around the room.

Larian was not just a Warrior Of The First Order, he had been made a Commander, and the achievement at such a young age assured him a future of wealth and prestige. The thought that this brilliant young man would wed his daughter was the answer to a fervent prayer; not only would she finally be married to an eminently suitable candidate, the union would cement relations between Verdana and Zanderone.

The Zanderone forces, though small in number, were highly skilled, and had been instrumental in Handerah's many victories; his alliance with the realm was of distinct importance, but he had a major concern.

Just as the marriage would solidify relations between the two realms, a breakup of the marriage could do irreparable harm, and he knew all to well that Lizbett was very difficult. If he gave his blessing and all was well, it would be a triumph, but if he gave his blessing and things did not work out...

He shook his head as he paced; it was a dilemma. He needed the young warrior to understand how willful Lizbett could be, that he would have to either tolerate her whims and fancies, or take a very hard line, and Lizbett did not do well under a hard line; he knew, he'd tried, oh, how he'd tried.

When he'd locked her in her room she'd climbed out the window, and risking life and limb she'd made her way across the slippery castle roof to one of the turrets. The guards were so shocked to see her they didn't know what to do, and when she told them she'd have them thrown in the dungeon if they breathed a word, it made their plight even more problematic. The King did not take kindly to having his troops put in such an untenable position.

There was his futile attempt to make her ride as a Princess should; he'd told Tholl to hide away the saddles except for the one she was supposed to use, but to Tholl's shock and horror she had simply jumped on her mare bareback with only a rope around the horse's neck, and had galloped away.

The alarm was raised, and Handerah was forced to send out his mounted guard to look for her, fearful that she'd come to harm riding in such a dangerous manner. After several hours and no success he realized she'd only be found if she chose to be, and it was a short time after the soldiers had been called back that she came trotting up the lane, as if she'd not a care in the world.

It seemed to Handerah, every time he attempted to clip her wings, the Princess would take flight regardless, and in a way that put her safety in jeopardy. It had become easier...and almost less of a worry...to leave her to her willful ways.

The King was fully aware that Lizbett had grown close to Larian during the summer of his training in the stables, and when he'd received Larian's letter asking for an audience to reacquaint himself with Lizbett with an eye to a courtship, it was obvious the fondness the young warrior felt for her still existed.

Would that be enough to hold the pair together if Lizbett threw one of her terrible temper tantrums? Did Larian have the patience to deal with her?

I must not keep him waiting any longer. I will simply tell him the truth. It's all I can do. Perhaps he's the man that can make Lizbett behave. I do hope so.

Still pondering he walked back to his throne, settled in, then signaled for the page to open the door. He was leaning back in the large, impressive chair when Commander Larian Lobergene entered the room, and the King almost caught his breath; Larian looked every bit the acclaimed warrior.

His tall, square-shouldered frame and heavily muscled body would intimidate any man, and the square jaw and piercing aqua eyes gave his face strength and character.

"Your Majesty," he murmured dropping to one knee.

"Larian Lobergene, please rise."

Larian slowly straightened up, and though the King was a powerful presence himself, Larian's energy seemed to fill the room.

"Let us retire to my study, we have much to discuss."

"As you wish, Sire," Larian replied with a slight bow of his head.

As the King moved from his throne and made his way to a side door, Larian kept his eyes downcast as a mark of respect. It did not go unnoticed, and it made clear to Handerah that in spite of his accomplishments Larian had remained humble.

"Please, let us not be formal," Handerah said warmly, pointing to a chair.

There were several thickly padded, tapestried chairs set in a semicircle in front of a massive fireplace in which a small amount of wood was burning. As Larian moved towards it, the flames gave the gold and silver threads of his burgundy vest a particularly eye-catching sparkle.

"I understand that vest is given when you achieve the rank of Warrior Of The First Order," Handerah remarked. "It is impressive."

"Thank you, Sire," Larian replied as he sat down. "It is one of several that I received with the vest itself. It resembles the true vest very closely, but the true vest is much thicker, and is adorned with precious stones, and nuggets of gold and silver, not just colored thread. It is kept in a locked cabinet, and can only be worn only on days of great importance, for example, my wedding day," he smiled.

"Ah, yes," Handerah nodded. "The reason for your visit."

"It is, yes, and I don't know if you are aware, but I ran across Lizbett on my way here. We spent some time together at the waterfall."

"I did receive a report that the two of you arrived at the castle together. I was surprised, but now I understand how that came about. What a lucky coincidence."

"Yes, I was delighted. It was quite the reunion," Larian commented thinking back to the naughty girl across his knee. "Your daughter has grown into a beauty."

"She has, but she can be a like a beautiful storm, all winds and tumult. It would give her mother and me the greatest joy to grant our permission for the two of you to wed, but you must understand she is headstrong and willful. I have done my best, Larian, but I had an easier time controlling the most headstrong member of my cabinet than I did Lizbett. She can be a very determined and difficult young woman."

Larian sighed. He knew exactly the jeopardy a marriage with Lizbett could pose and why the King was concerned.

"May I be frank, Sire?" Larian asked quietly, leaning forward in his chair as if he was about to relay a national secret.

"Please, yes, absolutely," Handerah replied, also leaning forward, drawn in my Larian's demeanor.

"I have seen glimpses of Lizbett's petulance and stubbornness, and I believe, given time, she can be directed to mend her ways."

"Really?" Handerah said his eyes wide in surprise.

"When one enters the warrior ranks, there is much that is taught. While there is emphasis on fighting skills, horsemanship, survival, and these types of things, there is also solemn and serious tutelage in the ways of men and women. Warriors may be strong and have physical expertise on the battlefield, he may be able to wield a sword with precision and power, but a woman can bring that same warrior to his knees."

"Yes, this is so, this is very true," Handerah agreed vehemently, "and Lizbett is such a woman. She is so beautiful, and such a...such a challenge, I have seen her do it. She has reduced some of her suitors into fury, others to great sadness. A slim young woman does possess such power over strong, brawny, brilliant men, I have seen it."

"I'm sure you have," Larian smiled. "I have been taught how to deal with such a woman, not with cruelty or brutality, but with wit, gentle but strong methods, and exerting a will stronger than hers. It takes time and finesse, but I have the time, and I believe the education, and of course, I care for her deeply."

"You have put my mind at ease," Handerah sighed, "and I thank you. I can feel these are not just words, that you have this tutelage you speak of. We should have such training here, but alas, I know of no man who is capable of such things."

"You do now," Larian smiled, "which brings me to the second matter, with your permission?"

"Yes, yes, of course. What is the second matter?"

"Lizbett will one day be Queen of Verdana, and at that time I will be required to stay with her."

"Ah, yes, this is so," the King nodded solemnly, embarrassed he'd not considered the problem himself.

"If I may be so bold, I would like to suggest something that will make this reasonable for me."

"Please, yes."

"Back in Zanderone, I am a Commander. I have already been given permission by my Prince to offer some of our training techniques to your men. If you would bestow the same rank to me here, it would give me position and bearing, I could train and teach, and when Lizbett takes the throne it would be an easy move up to become Commander General of Verdana's forces."

"Larian, that is an excellent proposal."

"I'm so pleased you think so, Sire. Now there is one final thing I must ask."

"Please, feel free."

"In order for me to channel Lizbett's fiery spirit, it would be best to have her stay at my residence. It is not a castle, but it is extremely comfortable, it has a full staff and is very secure. You can trust that I will not consummate our union until our wedding night, and that wedding will only happen when I have determined that Lizbett is the elegant, strong, compassionate woman we both know she can be. If I fail in that task, then I am not the one to be her life-mate."

"This is a highly irregular request, but I believe I understand the necessity. If she remained here she would have the safety net of my chambers, or her mother's. Alone with you…"

"Yes, Sire, exactly, but please know, if I fear I am being ineffective I will escort her back here immediately."

"I must consult with my wife, but I have no objection. I see the wisdom behind the request, and I trust you, Larian."

"I am honored that you do, Sire, and I thank you. I have already had a few words with Lizbett, and I believe at dinner tonight you might see a slight change."

"Already? You've only just arrived," the King declared.

"Indeed," Lairan smiled. "I do request, though, that we not be seated together."

"I don't understand."

"I have told Lizbett that to sit next to me is a privilege that must be earned."

The Monarch paused, staring at him for a moment, then broke into a broad grin.

"Ah, you are a clever man," he remarked, "I will see to it."

"Thank you, Sire. The initial stages of, if you'll pardon the expression, taming the naughty woman, can be very effective. It's the middle part of her journey that can be challenging, when she realizes it's no longer a game, that the expectation is not a temporary one."

"This is when it is important that she be away from here."

"Yes, Sire."

"Hmmm, there is one element…"

"You look worried."

"It's the journey. You'll have to cross over the barren land. There are marauders there. Our peace is tenuous. I'm worried for her safety."

"I have a special carriage on its way here Sire, and I hope you will forgive the presumption, but I thought it better to have it ready should we forge this agreement. The carriage is equipped with a secret compartment in which she can hide should it be necessary, and accompanied by a retinue of my best warriors who will, naturally, accompany us on our return. These marauders flee when faced with skilled men such as mine, and only attack if they see something they want, or need, and if she is hidden away…"

"They are scavengers at best," Handerah nodded. "As long as she is out of sight they will have no will to fight just for the sake of it."

"Exactly," Larian nodded. "The carriage is filled with foodstuffs, gifts from the Prince to you and your good wife. I doubt they will fight for such fare, and this is excellent training for my men. Diplomacy, the ability to negotiate out of a fight is part of their training. They are tasked with arriving here without having raised a sword."

"And that is the excuse for the carriage to be coming here, a gift for me in thanks for the banquet in your honor."

"Should the men have to show the contents of the carriage, yes, so it will make sense that it will be empty on the return trip. I have fought these marauders, Sire. I was able to take on several at once and depart without a scratch. This is why I have no concern about them."

"I am reassured, Larian," the King declared.

"Then I will await final word after you have spoken to your wife. Thank you, Sire, I believe Lizbett and I will have a very long and contented life, at least, if we are married."

"Getting her under control before walking her down the path to the arch of the ceremony."

"Yes, Sire, once we are there all will be well."

"This has been an excellent meeting," the King declared, "and I believe, for the first time in many passes of the moons, I will be sleeping much more easily where my daughter is concerned."

"I'm glad, Sire, and I am honored and grateful for your blessing."

"You know," said Handerah as he walked Larian to the door, "I believe you will be successful with Lizbett for one very important reason.

"What's that Sire?"

"She cares for you deeply. Were that not the case, I'm not sure your training would matter."

"Sire, you are wise indeed, and you are absolutely correct."

CHAPTER SIX

L izbett had chosen a pale green gown studded with precious jewels, and had sparkling threads woven into the locks in her long red hair. Dabbing on the powder that would bring her cheeks and lips to a bright red, she smiled at her image in the reflecting glass.

"He will be sorry not to be sitting next to me now," she giggled.

Lizbett was particular about her dress, and couldn't abide even the slightest wrinkle or spot on anything; making one last check of her gown to make sure it was completely pristine, she rose from her chair and headed to the banquet hall.

As the guest of honor Larian was to be seated next to the King, and Lizbett would have been on Larian's other side, but with the warrior's request Handerah hadn't been sure where to place her, then he realized with his wife away she could sit in her mother's chair next to him.

All eyes were upon her as she entered the banquet hall, and she smiled happily as she heard the complimentary comments about her dress and overall beauty. It didn't surprise her, she was used to such attention, and glided forward to the head table where the page showed her where she would be sitting.

"In my mother's chair, but where will Larian be?" she murmured as she sat down. "Perhaps I will be next to him after all."

There were three tables in all; two long ones facing each other, then the King's table at the head between the two of them with six chairs. Three permanent places for the King, his wife, and Lizbett, with the remaining three for visiting dignitaries.

Handerah's chair was larger than the rest, and Lizbett's hope that she'd be next to Larian began to wane; she suspected Larian would be next to the King on his other side. She frowned. It would have been much easier to catch his eye if here were anywhere but there.

The Head Of The Court had been waiting for the Princess to arrive, and when she was finally in her chair he pounded his large wooden stake on the floor; it alerted everyone that the King was about to enter and they were to stand.

In the chamber next to the banquet room Handerah and Larian had been sharing some wine and special tidbits of food made especially for the two of them. It was a men's only area, and while there were times the King would have other members of his court join him, tonight he had only Larian as his guest.

The tidbits of food were being served by two topless maidens who considered it an honor to be chosen for the task. When The Head Of the Court would discreetly put out the word that he was searching for new girls to serve the King and his guests in the chamber before a banquet, he had more applicants than he could interview. The final list was limited to twelve, and it was often by personal recommendations that the young maidens would be fortunate enough to find themselves standing naked from the waist up under the scrutinizing eye of The Head Of The Court.

His name was Farris, and he had been a servant of Handerah's for many years. The hopeful maidens would stand in his office, and he would move down the line, studying their overall demeanor before plucking at the ripe cherries topping their breasts. He would calculate how quickly the nipples puckered, for how long they stayed stiff, and lastly, how the girl reacted. Beautiful breasts were a prerequisite, but the maiden had to have a sweetness and purity about her in order to serve in the chamber off the banquet room.

The practice was well-known and accepted by all. The girls might be toyed with, but their honor was left in tact, and since they were from the modest villages it gave them an opportunity to meet men above their station. It wasn't a far-fetched notion that they might be serving their future husband; nobles had no quarrel about marrying girls from the village, finding them grateful and eager to please.

The King had requested one of his favorite maidens, a girl named Starling. She was a fair-haired, comely beauty with bounteous breasts, a mischievous smile, and a look that suggested she was up for more than a little breast fondling. Larian had been partnered with a brown-haired girl named Falayla, who had no such demeanor; she was subdued and appeared almost delicate.

The men were seated in wide armless chairs, and as Falayla brought forth another dish of delicacies, she perched herself on Larian's lap. Starling had been on and off Handerah's knee several times, and Larian guessed Falayla had finally found the nerve to follow suit.

"Would you like me to feed you, Sir?" she asked softly.

"Certainly," Larian replied, and as he opened his mouth the young maiden dropped the bite-sized morsel on to his tongue. "Mmm, that is delicious," he smiled.

"Would you care to fondle my breasts, Sir?"

Larian chuckled. He was well aware of the customs of Handerah's court, and while he didn't object he knew it was something in which he would not indulge once married.

"Do they not please you?" she asked.

"They are very attractive," he said warmly, and raising his hand fondled one of her luscious mounds, then the other, lightly pinching her nipples.

"Oh, Sir, your touch," she quivered, closing her eyes.

"What about my touch, tell me," he said dropping his voice.

"It is strong, yet…yet…oooh, Sir, it is strong but so tender."

"I think that is enough," he decreed dropping his hand away.

"Sir, if I may say," she sighed fluttering open her eyes, "you could touch me that way for a full passage of the moons and I would still ask for more."

The sound of the Head Of The Court pounding his stake on the floor broke into the intimate moment, and moving Starling off his lap the King rose from his chair.

"That was an excellent beginning to our evening," he declared. "I trust you enjoyed the pleasure of my banquet chamber."

"I did, Sire, thank you," Larian nodded as he began to gently moved Falayla from his lap.

"Sir?" she squeaked sporting a worried frown.

"Yes, Falayla?"

"I…uh…" she mumbled, but her face crinkled as she attempted to suppress a wash of tears.

Larian stared at her; something was terribly wrong, and the girl was having great difficulty finding the words to tell him what it was.

"Starling, Falayla, you go and enjoy your meal now. You know where it is served," the King said firmly. "Falayla, off his lap."

Though Larian wanted to uncover the cause of the maiden's distress, his obligation was to the King, but as Falayla dropped her head in resignation and slid off his lap he promised himself he'd return at the end of the meal to determine her trouble.

The two girls curtsied and disappeared behind a heavy dark green curtain at the end of the room, and doing his best to shake the girl from his thoughts, Larian followed the King to the door that would take them into the banquet.

"Are you ready to face your adoring public?" Handerah smiled.

"I am, Sire," Larian replied, *but there is only one I truly look forward to seeing, only one whose eyes I wish to see gaze up at me.*

Farris banged his stick one more time; it meant all had risen and it was time for the King to enter. Lizbett stared at the door, knowing that a bare-breasted maiden would have been serving Larian, and praying that she had not turned his head.

"Stop worrying," she muttered to herself. "You are a Princess. A mere village girl would not cause him to change his affection for you," but in spite of her argument she remained unconvinced.

As the door opened and Larian walked into the room, she glanced around and saw every woman, married or not, gaze at him.

His height, his broad shoulders, the shimmering burgundy vest and white shirt barely covering the muscles underneath, the man that was Lord Larian Lobergene was taking their collective breath away. His hair, though no longer hanging in golden ringlets as it had when they were younger, was still curling around his handsome features highlighting his aqua eyes.

I must be on my very best behavior. I cannot have another stealing him away. I cannot.

As the page ushered Handerah and Larian to their seats, Larian smiled across at her and sent her a covert look; it was a look that touched her heart, that made the area between her legs warm and moist, but it was also a look that said, *I'll be watching you.*

The guests stood waiting; no-one was permitted to sit before the King had settled into his throne, and he had chosen to remain standing; it meant he was going to say a few words about the man for whom the banquet was being held.

"Friends of the Court of Verdana," he began, "I honor my guest this evening, Lord Larian Lobergene from the Principality of our most treasured neighbors, the Zanderonians. These great people have fought side-by-side with our forces, ensuring our many victories, and it is with great pride I welcome Lord Larian to my court. He was named Warrior of the First Order, but an even greater title was bestowed upon him. He was named

46

Commander and given his own retinue of men, the youngest warrior ever to have ever achieved such status."

A murmur ran through the crowd, and Lizbett, shocked at the news, leaned forward attempting to see him better. Her stable boy, her Larian, was a Commander! A quiver of pride and lust shivered down her spine; it was no wonder his authority had overcome her.

"Please raise your goblets and welcome our most revered guest, and join me in congratulating him on his accomplishments. To Lord Larian!"

The crowd repeated the name, making it sound like a chant, then lifted their goblets and drank. As was the custom Larian waited until all the goblets were back on the table, then began to speak.

"I am humbled and touched by this warm welcome, and I thank the King most humbly for having me here as his guest. I bring greetings from my Prince, and am to report that there is a carriage on its way bringing some delicacies from my realm which I hope you will all enjoy. If I may, I would like at this time to ask that you raise your goblets and toast your mighty monarch, a man known to be both fierce and fair, King Handerah!"

The crowd raised their drinks, chanted the King's name, and drank. It was only then that the King sat down, which allowed everyone else to follow suit, and the feast began.

But Lizbett wasn't hungry. She wanted to behave, but she wanted Larian to see her behave, and she also wanted him to see her in all her finery.

How can I do this? I can't get up and parade around, I can't even leave my seat until we have finished with this soup being served. Oh, I don't want to wait, I want him to see me now. What to do...what to do...maybe I could offer another toast, but it's probably too late. I must think of something.

A bowl of the steaming brew was placed before her, and lifting her spoon she was about to take a sip when a subtle but distinct aroma tickled her nostrils; instantly she knew something wasn't right.

Urgently she looked at her father and tugged at his sleeve, but he was so busy engaged in conversation with Larian he ignored her. Trying to calm the pounding in her heart she stared down at the bowls in front of both him and Larian, and saw that neither of them had yet picked up their spoons.

"Father," she whispered, tugging on his sleeve more aggressively.

Still he did not respond, and when she saw Larian lift his spoon she knew what she had to do.

As quickly but as discreetly as possible she slipped from her chair, hurried behind her father's throne, and just as Larian was about to raise the spoon to his lips she touched his shoulder, causing him to pause

"Lizbett?" he frowned.

Dropping her lips to his ear she whispered,

"I fear the soup may be poisoned, at the very least tainted. I could smell it. Please, I promise you, I am not pretending."

He stared to her violet eyes, and he could see her fear.

"Lizbett? What is the meaning of this?" her father demanded in a hushed but angry tone.

"Thank you," Larian smiled at her. "I will handle this. Please return to your seat."

She wanted to hug him, to kiss him, to fall beside him and thank him for believing her, but she knew such a display would have to wait, and she hurried back to her chair.

"Sire," Larian said softly to Handerah as she left, "it is possible there may be foul play at work…with the contents of your bowl. I see the guests at the other tables seem to be taking it and have no problem, but I believe Lizbett when she says she is worried."

A heavy frowned crossed Handerah's brow.

"Did she say how she knew?" the King asked softly.

"She said she could smell it," Larian replied.

"This is not widely known," he sighed, "but she has been gifted with her mother's keen sense of smell. We must be very careful how we proceed."

"If it was placed in her bowl it may well have been placed in yours as well. With your wife away, should something happen to you, the Kingdom would be vulnerable…perhaps it was also placed in mine to cause even further chaos, maybe even start a rift between Verdana and Zanderone."

"Such evil," Handerah frowned. "How to proceed? This is the question."

"If we pretend to fall ill, perhaps the guilty party might make himself known," Larian suggested.

"Perhaps, but that will take time, and there's no guarantee that the man who steps forward is not doing so to save the realm, not harm it further. No, there is another way, and I believe that rests with my daughter."

"Lizbett?"

"We must pretend we are not supping the soup because we are drinking and eating the breads and cheeses. In a moment you are going to make a grand gesture and ask Lizbett to dance to entertain the crowd, then you will escort her out of the room, ostensibly to have a quiet moment, but you will whisk her into the kitchen and she can put her nose to work. She will be able to smell who is carrying the poison. It will be an easy task to get the truth from that person before the powers behind him have any idea."

"Sire, I do see risk, but I believe it is the best course of action. Let us clink our goblets and eat the bread, then I will fetch Lizbett and take her to dance."

They laughed and joked as they raised their drinks, and Lizbett knew they'd quickly formed a plan. Much relieved she reached for some bread herself, covertly glancing around the room.

Was anyone watching them? Was someone eager for them to sup the soup? She saw nothing, but if her father had a plan she was confident the guilty party would soon be uncovered.

CHAPTER SEVEN

As Larian moved Lizbett across the dance floor he whispered the plan, and when the musicians came to the end of the song they bowed before the crowd, then taking her hand he led her from the room. There were whispers and giggles, and while the King was smiling broadly he was darting his eyes at the faces before him; in their midst were traitors, but he couldn't fathom who or why.

Lizbett hurried Larian down the empty passageways to the kitchen. It wasn't far, sitting just behind the banquet room chamber, and as she was about to burst through the door Larian stopped her.

"You walk around the kitchen, as though casually giving me a tour, and when you smell the culprit don't say anything, just show me with your eyes then leave the rest to me."

"But I-"

"Lizbett!"

"Sorry, yes, Larian, I'll do as you say."

Taking a deep breath she pushed open the heavy door and moved inside. A thousand fragrances washed through her, but nothing distasteful, nothing that smelled like the tangy foul thing that had alerted her. She began to move slowly around the large kitchen, smiling and nodding as the cooks and servants did their work, but still she could not detect the aroma.

Was I mistaken? Was there no such smell? No, I'm sure I...

Her thoughts were abruptly interrupted by the vaguest scent, and it was wafting from the alcove that led into the chamber. Larian was behind her, and turning she looked up at him, then nodded her head towards the door.

Not sure what might lay in wait on the other side, he moved in front of her, pulled the latch and allowed the door to swing open; to his surprise there was only Falayla and Starling, still bare-breasted, seated at a small table eating their meal. Without warning Lizbett swiftly moved past him; her nose had detected the aroma and it was leading her directly to Falayla.

Almost upon her, Lizbett wanted to grab the girl by the hair and drag her from the room; she wanted to slap her and call her every name that came to mind.

"Princess!" Larian called sharply, causing her to stop and spin around to face him.

"Larian, it's-"

His aqua eyes glinted across at her, his message clear, *stop and come back here at once.*

Starling stared at them both, confusion written across her face, but when Larian glanced at Falayla all he saw was fear, guilt and shame. He flashed back to the moment just before he and Handerah had entered the banquet hall; she had wanted to warn him but terror had gripped her.

He could see Lizbett was still fighting her rage and moved quickly to her side.

"Lizbett, would you please return to the banquet," he whispered urgently in her ear. "Be sure to be all smiles. Tell your father what has transpired, and make sure knows that I'll be back to join him very soon."

Her need to remain and interrogate the culprit surged through her, and she stared at him intently, silently pleading with him to let her stay, but his resolve was unyielding.

"Go," he said firmly. "I will deal with this."

Realizing any argument was futile she frowned angrily, and was about to march away when Larian smiled down at her.

"Lizbett, you saved the day," he breathed. "Now keep your head, smile, act happy, don't alert anyone. There is evil afoot and it will be watching."

She took a deep breath, and sighing heavily she nodded her understanding.

"I know what to do," she replied, and hurried from the room, closing the door behind her.

"Sir, what is all this? Is there something wrong?" Starling asked completely bewildered.

"I just need a private word with Falayla," he replied calmly, "but you may continue your meal. Falayla, if you would please step on the other side of the curtain with me?"

He could see her dread, and as she attempted to rise from the table she was unsteady on her feet.

"It's all right, I'm sure you have been badly used," he said softly as he reached out to help her, and wrapping his muscled arm around her shoulder he allowed her to fall against him. "Starling, do not leave this room. If anyone asks where Falayla has gone, no matter who it is, you tell them she had to leave for a moment but you don't know where. This is extremely important, do you understand?"

Starling gazed at the handsome warrior. Whatever was going on she didn't care; she'd do whatever he said.

"Yes, Sir, I understand. You can count on me."

"Thank you," he smiled warmly, and supporting Falayla he led her through the curtain and across to a grouping of chairs on the other side of the chamber, far enough away so Starling would not be able to hear their private murmurings.

"First, you have my word I will protect you," he assured the frightened girl as he sat next to her on a settee. "I am sure you have been scared for days. Am I right?"

"So scared, Sir, so, so scared," she whimpered, the tears beginning to cascade down her face.

"Please, be strong now. You're safe, you must tell me everything."

"It was Farris," she blubbered trying to compose herself. "When he picked me out of the girls for serving today, I was so surprised because I'm not like the other maidens. I'm shy, I didn't really want to-"

"What did he say, what did he do?" Larian said urgently.

"It wasn't just him. There were three other men with him, and they stood around me. They...they...oh, the shame of it," she sobbed.

"Tell me, quickly," he pressed. "We have so little time before he comes to find you. He will have you try again."

"I'm sorry...they told me if I didn't do what they said they would each have me, both back and front," she whispered, "but even then I refused. I would never hurt the King, never. You must believe me."

"I do," Larian assured her. "Keep going."

"So then they said if I didn't do their bidding they would do the same to my mother, and my little sister, and they would kill my father and burn my family's home. It was so terrible," she sobbed, and overcome she dropped her head in her hands.

"He is a fiend," Larian hissed. "Please, Falayla, take hold, I will protect you and your family."

"But he has soldiers at my home," she quivered. "If I do not carry out his orders..."

"Who were the other three men? Do you know?"

"I don't know their names, but they're here. They are all sitting together with their wives. They're at the end of the table with Farris. The wives, I just remembered, I heard the men say their wives would have sport with the Queen when she returned."

"What else?" he pressed.

"Um, a guard named Crellus, or Crullis, something like that, had a few men on his side, and that's all they would need, just a few men."

"This is so evil," he growled.

"I almost drank the poison myself," she declared, "so they couldn't make me hurt the King, and the Princess…but then I feared for my family."

Larian stared into her red, tear-filled eyes, and knew she spoke the truth; she would have taken her own life before killing the King, and would have but for her loved ones.

"Do you want to make this right? Do you want to help save the King now?"

"I have wanted to save the King," she replied, her face crinkled with sincerity.

"Think, Falayla, since we did not partake of the soup, will he ask you to try again with another serving?"

"He already has, in the gravy," she said slowly, "everything else is being taken out on big platters. He can't use the cake, that will be part of the ceremony."

"The ceremony! I'd forgotten about the ceremony. This is excellent. How did you put the poison in the soup?"

"When the server brought out the soup for the head table, I was supposed to take the tray and send him back to the kitchen for another bottle of wine and pour it in then, but I couldn't bring myself to do it."

"I don't understand, didn't you put in the bowls."

"I opened the vial and a tiny drop fell into one of them, but only because my hand was shaking. When I couldn't do it I thought I was condemning my family to a horrible death," she whimpered, a fresh wave of tears spilling down her face.

"Falaya, you poor girl. What did you tell Farris?"

"That the boy came back with the wine before I had a chance. That's when he said I was to pour it into your gravy boat."

"So, you still have the vial?"

"Yes, I have two of them," she replied pulling them from the folds of her skirt. "He gave me two in case I dropped one, or spilled it or something."

"Excellent. Can you be brave for me? Just for a little while? I promise your family will come to no harm but you must do exactly as I say."

"I will, Sir, I will," she vowed.
"Good, now listen carefully."

CHAPTER EIGHT

B ack at the King's table Lizbett had relayed the information, and Handerah laughed and joked as if she had just told him something highly amusing. When he saw Larian appear through the door from the chamber and whisk Farris from his seat to speak to him away from the other guests, Handerah was immediately filled with concern, but when he saw Farris grin and nod his head it was clear Larian was just being amicable, pretending nothing was awry.

Good, Larian, make jokes, act as though all is well. We can't trust anyone, not even Farris, though I am tempted. He knows all the nobles intimately, he may have heard rumblings.

Handerah was eager to learn what Larian had discovered from the duplicitous maiden, but the warrior was talking with Farris at length. The King could see Farris was becoming somewhat restless, shifting his weight from one foot to the other, as though he needed to sit back down or had some pressing business. When Larian finally left him the King saw Farris frown deeply, then dart inside the banquet chamber.

Ambling slowly back to his chair, Larian settled next to the King and with a wide grin began to relay all the information he'd gathered; Handerah was aghast.

"What are we to do?" Handerah groaned.

"I have already hatched the counter attack, Sire," Larian assured him. "You need not fear. No harm can come to any of us, at least not from poison, not tonight, but the plotters, they have an unfortunate end coming their way. This is what I have planned. If it meets with your approval I will do nothing. If it does not, it can be stopped."

Quickly but in great detail Larian outlined his scheme, and when he finished Handerah nodded in agreement, then let out a heavy sigh.

"It is an excellent plan. It's no wonder your Prince made you a Commander. You are not just cunning, you are insightful. It saddens me greatly that Farris would wish to do me harm, it is stunning news, but you're right, he must be dealt with. I owe you my life, Larian."

"It is Lizbett to whom we are indebted, Sire. Were it not for her nose…"

"Yes, my beautiful, willful daughter," he said warmly, turning to face her.

Lizbett had been sitting quietly, too unnerved by what had happened to do anything. She wanted to be next her father, to feel the power of the throne; sensing her trepidation the King leaned in and whispered in her ear.

"All is well, child. Do not fear, this will soon be over, sooner than you might expect."

"Thank you, father. I do confess to feeling quite shaken."

"You have a small task to perform. Are you up to it?"

"Of course," she nodded, feigning a bravery she did not feel.

"It's quite simple," he smiled, and leaning in, whispered the instruction in her ear.

"Sire," Larian said softly, recapturing the King's attention when he'd finished talking to Lizbett, "you must keep her in sight. If there are other culprits not yet uncovered they may still try to take her. They may see her as a way out, a bargaining chip."

"Yes, yes, you're right, Larian. Never fear, until this business is over she will stay in my apartments."

"I must send an urgent message to my Prince. If there is danger here, there may be danger in Zanderone as well. We do not know the extent of this treachery."

"Yes, yes. When the ceremony is over. We must wait until then," the King said solemnly. "Do you see that man, the one in the brown leather?" Handerah asked, nodding his head to the table opposite the one at which the plotters were seated.

"Yes, I see him."

"He is the Commander of my personal guard, Lockley. He is drinking heavily. I don't believe he would be downing so many goblets if he was involved. He would be watching, pretending to drink."

"I agree, Sire, the man is happily at ease, it's obvious."

"You said the maiden named someone called Curullis?"

"Yes, Sire."

"It must be Corilleus. There is no love lost between Corilleus and Lockley. When Lizbett has her accident, you must go to Lockley and tell him what's happening. He is to slip away, find Corilleus and arrest him, and anyone with him. We can sort out the innocent from the guilty quickly enough."

"This is a good plan," Larian agreed. "No-one will think anything of me saying hello to a fellow warrior, especially your personal guard."

"He must also send five of his most trusted men back here immediately to wait outside the doors for my call."

During their exchange large platters of meat and fowl had been set upon the tables, along with boats of gravy; the King, Lizbett and Larian were sharing a single gravy bowl between them. The King was plating some meat, and Larian some fowl, when reaching for the wine bottle Lizbett 'accidentally' knocked the gravy bowl, sending it crashing to the floor. Handerah covertly glanced at Farris; the man's face was ten shades of purple.

As the servants hurried to the table to clean up the mess, Larian used it as the excuse to wander across to introduce himself to Lockley. Meanwhile, back at the King's table Lizbett told the servants to fetch the gravy boat that Farris and his three accomplices had been using.

"Ah, thank you," Lizbett smiled, pouring the gravy across her meat.

Things settled back down, and the meal continued with some jesters juggling and some acrobats bouncing between the tables for entertainment. Every time Handerah glanced over at Farris and his cohorts, he saw only forced smiles and furrowed brows. When the platters and plates were finally cleared away and the entertainers had left the room the King rose to his feet.

"Friends of the court, may I have your attention!"

A hush fell across the crowd, and a table was carried in and placed in the center of the room where the entertainers had just been performing.

"As is the custom, our honored guest will serve you all," he announced as a large cake was brought in and placed on the table. "With Lord Larian being such a swordsman, I'm sure the pieces will be equal."

There was laughter and tittering in the crowd, and Larian rose from his chair.

"Thank you, Sire, it will be my great pleasure."

Moving from his chair he strode to the table, lifted the thin, glimmering knife, and sliced through the middle of the large, square dessert. There was applause as he sliced off two pieces and presented them to the King and Lizbett.

"Prepare yourselves," he muttered as he laid them down. "Sire, if you please."

Handerah waited until Larian had returned to the table and was slicing more pieces, before once again rising from his chair.

"Friends of the Court, I have an announcement, and it seems appropriate to make it while Lord Larian is slicing the cake."

Though his head was down, Larian's eyes were not focused on his task, they were glancing across at Farris and his cronies; as he'd hoped the traitors and their wives were staring up at the King; it would have been rude to look anywhere else. Covertly retrieving the tiny vial of poison from the pocket of his vest, he dropped its contents upon the small slices of cake, keeping one untainted.

"Commander Larian will not just be a Commander for his Principality of Zanderone, he has agreed to share his experience and knowledge with us, and will be sworn in as a Commander here in Verdana."

He balanced the four plates of cake along the length of each of his muscled arms, and as he carried them across to Farris and his comrades there was a smattering of applause and calls of congratulations. Carefully placing the dishes in front of each of them, he straightened himself up and gave a small bow to the crowd.

"When you receive your cake," the King declared, "please eat heartily to show your support of our new Commander."

With Larian standing directly in front of them the group were obliged to lift their forks and eat, and it was only a moment later that the commotion began.

Farris and his friends began choking, grabbing at their throats, some banging the table with their fists. Within seconds all but one of the eight was on the floor or leaning back in their chair with white foam spilling from their mouth.

"No-one move!" the King commanded.

With lightening speed Larian reached across, grabbed the sole, stunned survivor by his jacket, and lifting him easily, he yanked him over the table and flung on the floor in front of the King's table. Falling into a crumpled, terrified heap, the once proud noble stared up at his monarch.

"Mercy, Sire, mercy," he cried.

"Friends of the Court," the King bellowed ignoring the pleading man and raising his voice over the panic in the room. "Farris and his friends just attempted to poison me, the Princess, and Lord Larian. Now that poison has been turned against them. No-one will leave this room until I determine it is safe for you to do so. There may be others waiting to do you harm."

The truth was, not only did Handerah want the opportunity to interrogate each of them personally, with one of the plotters left alive he would quickly learn who else was involved and he didn't want anyone to leave the room.

"Guards!"

The banquet doors flew open and five fully suited warriors strode forward.

"Two of you, take this man to the dungeons. You, guard this door to the banquet chamber, you two, stay by the banquet doors. No-one is to come in or leave."

With the situation firmly in hand, Larian hurried to Lizbett's side.

"Larian, I can't believe it," she breathed, her eyes wide.

"Everything is in hand," he said calmly. "There's something I have to do, but I will be back before the moon's are high."

"No," she protested, "please, you can't leave me."

"You're staying with your father until I return. I made a promise and it's one I must keep."

"A promise? A promise to who?" she quivered. "Surely I am more important."

"I'll tell you everything when I return, but I must go. Be brave for me, and do whatever your father says."

"I will," she said, giving up, her face crumpling. "I wish you weren't going."

"I must, but soon I shall come to your father's chambers for you."

"Hurry, and be careful."

"I will."

Handerah had left the table and was staring down at the bodies of Farris and his coconspirators; Larian moved quickly to his side.

"I fear there are more," the King said ruefully.

"You will soon uncover them," Larian assured him.

"Now it has become imperative for you to take Lizbett to your home. I would ask, had you not already requested it."

"You're right, Sire. You cannot have her safety on your mind while dealing with this business."

"Exactly."

"I must escort Falayla back to her home, along with some soldiers, and make sure her family is safe. She is waiting for me behind the green curtain. I'm sure she is still very frightened. She has no idea what just transpired here."

"Yes, quickly. There will be four warriors at the stables, take them."

"Thank you, Sire. I told Lizbett I would call upon her at your private apartment when I return."

"I will be anxious to know what transpired, so we will both be waiting eagerly for your return."

"Thank you, Sire. I will be quick."

"Terrible business," the King muttered as Larian turned quickly away and headed into the chamber to fetch Falayla. "Terrible."

CHAPTER NINE

It wasn't until the moons were high in the sky that Larian returned to the castle. It had taken some time for him and the four guards to reach the hamlet where Falayla's family lived, and when they arrived at the small house they found no guards. The family was perfectly safe, and were completely unaware of the drama their precious daughter had endured.

"You poor child," her mother cried pulling her into her arms. "What a dreadful man he must have been."

"Your daughter did the King a great service tonight, and will be rewarded," Larian promised. "Just to be cautious I'm leaving two guards here to watch over you. They'll stay until it is deemed safe for them to leave."

"We're most thankful, Sir," Falayla's father said humbly. "Our children are our treasure, and we are so grateful you brought her safely home."

As Larian had ridden back to the castle he'd spotted a man fleeing through the dark, obviously one of Farris's cohorts who had managed to escape. It was a short scuffle and the guards soon had him secured, but Larian wanted to deliver him personally to Lockley to have him thrown in dungeon for questioning.

The moons had already begun their descent as Larian was finally hurrying through the castle, down the long passageways to the King's apartment. There were guards everywhere, security was tight, and as he approached the door he was halted before he could reach it.

"Lord Larian Lobergene. The King is expecting me."

They made him wait while another guard disappeared to check, and he was then escorted through the doors into the foyer where he saw more guards standing at attention.

"Larian, what news?" the King asked eagerly as he strode forward to greet him.

"The family was fine, there was no-one there. It was clear they knew nothing of the attempt on your life. The poor girl suffered for no reason. On the journey to her home though, she told me Farris did exactly what we anticipated; he took the vial from her and poured it into the gravy boat himself."

"How disappointed he must have been when Lizbett sent it flying to the floor," Handerah remarked.

"Did you see the look on his face?" Larian asked. "As hard as he tried he could not disguise it."

"I did," the King said grimly. "Even though the gravy no longer contained the poison it was still necessary. She was upset, her accident may not have been successful. Keeping him talking long enough for Falayla to empty the vial and fill it with water was very clever, Larian."

"Thank you, Sire. It was fortunate there was only the cake left to be served. There was no possibility of him tampering with that, but may I inquire, how are you? Is there any news?"

"I am weary, but I do not dare sleep. The interrogations continue and I must wait for the information. Oh, I was able to send an urgent messenger to your Prince."

"Sire, thank you. I was about to ask you how I might do that."

"It is imperative he know.'

"Yes, it is," Larian agreed. "I promised Lizbett I'd check on her, is she still awake?"

"I see her lamps still burning under the crack of her door. Her apartment is just down that hallway, but I'll walk with you. The guards won't let you near her otherwise."

"My carriage will be arriving tomorrow," Larian said as they headed down the wide corridor. "If I can switch out the horses we can leave right away."

"I think it would be best. Her mother will be back tomorrow after the suns have crossed. I don't want to worry about both of them."

"Have you told Lizbett I'll be taking her to my residence for her safety?"

"I have. She was excited, then worried about leaving me, then excited again. I'm sure she is still a bit perplexed, but it's for the best...for many reasons."

"Thank you, Sire," Larian said gratefully. "I won't bring it up now unless she does. I will talk with her more about it over the morning meal."

They had reached her door and Handerah opened it and gestured for him to enter.

"Larian, thank you again for all you have done tonight. You have proven you are worthy of all the titles you carry. Now please, go and put Lizbett's mind to rest. There is a bed chamber adjacent to hers, it's just through a heavy curtain. If you choose to stay you have my blessing. I would probably rest easier knowing you are near her, in spite of all her protection."

"Thank you, Sire. I shall give it some thought."

"She'll be through there," Handerah smiled, pointing at a doorway across the foyer. "I know she'll be very happy you're back safely. I'll see you when the suns rise."

Larian watched the large man stride away. Carrying the weight of the Kingdom on his shoulders was a heavy load, but he bore the burden well, and Larian had tremendous admiration for him.

Moving to the door of what he assumed would be Lizbett's bed chamber he knocked gently, and it was opened in an instant;

Lizbett, out of her formal gown and dressed in a long, cream robe, flung herself against him and hugged him tightly.

"Where have you been? What took so long? I've been so worried."

"Easy," he crooned, moving into the chamber and kicking the door closed with his foot. "I told you, I had-"

"I know, some promise to keep. What promise, what did you have to do?"

"I had to make sure Falayla was safely returned to her family," he said patiently.

"You put a common village girl before me?" Lizbett gasped pushing him away and staring up at him.

"That common village girl put her life on the line for you," he frowned. "Now stop this nonsense. I know it's been hard for you and you've been frightened, but you're alive and the devils have been captured, in no small part thanks to her."

"Hold me, Larian, please, you're right, I was frightened, so frightened. Please don't leave me again."

"Dear girl," he said, taking her hands, "your father has already requested I sleep in the bed chamber next to yours, and so I will."

"You won't sleep next to me? I would feel so much safer. Please?"

"No," he said firmly, "that would not be right, but I will be very close, and now, Lizbett, now I must spank you and reward you. Only you could warrant both."

"What do you mean?" she asked, her eyes staring at him disbelief. "How could you possibly wish to spank me on such a night as this?"

"I gave you strict instructions when we entered the banquet chamber and you completely ignored them," he scolded.

"But I knew it was her, I knew-"

"That is scarcely the point," he interjected taking her by the elbow and moving her to her large, canopied bed. "It was a delicate matter. I knew a maiden so young and innocent was merely a pawn. I needed to win her confidence so I could learn more."

"She poisoned my soup," Lizbett retorted.

"She did not. Now sit down and I'll tell you the truth of the matter, and please don't interrupt me," he said sternly, placing her on the edge of the mattress and sitting next to her.

Lizbett listened attentively as Larian explained the evil machinations that had been implemented by the devil Farris, and when he'd finished she let out a long sigh.

"So Falayla is to be rewarded," she remarked, "not condemned."

"Yes, but Lizbett, you too were brave tonight, and you saved us all."

"Then why would you wish to spank me?" she frowned. "I don't understand."

"You are overwrought, you are very..."

"Very what?" she frowned.

"Very...tight."

"What do you expect? People tried to kill us!"

"The kind of spanking I have in mind will give you a little punishment, such as you deserve for ignoring my instruction, but also take away all that tightness."

"It will? How is that possible?"

"Lay across my knee, Princess, and you will find out."

Lizbett stared into his eyes; she wanted to obey him, she also wanted to believe him, but she couldn't quite bring herself to do either.

"Why do you hesitate?"

"I don't know," she said, her brow crinkling.

"I think there are times you like to disobey just for the sake of it," he smiled.

She dropped her eyes and shifted her seat.

"Being strong doesn't mean you have to fight everything and everyone all the time. Being obedient doesn't make you weak. On the contrary, being obedient can show your strength. I obey my Prince and your father. Does that make me weak?"

"That's different," she quipped.

"Princess, you must lay over my knee and accept your spanking. If you do this now, right now, you will also be rewarded. If you do not, all you will end up with is a sore bottom."

"Larian," she whispered, "I...uh...okay..."

Sighing, she slowly moved across his thighs, wriggling to get comfortable, and rested her head on the mattress.

"I can't believe I'm doing this," she bleated.

"What? Being obedient for once?" he smiled.

"No, letting you spank me without...uh...protesting."

"I'm proud of you," he said tenderly, smoothing his hand over the smooth silk of the robe as it laid over her curves. "You're being a good girl. Because you complied I won't spank you as hard as I would have, and you'll be rewarded as well."

"I'm being stupid, letting you do this," she argued.

"Always with the debate! That is something I will spank out of you, I swear," he declared landing a sound swat.

"OUCH."

"That was for calling yourself stupid," he said sternly. "You may be many things, Princess, but stupid isn't one of them."

"Thank you...I think," she muttered.

"Now be still and no yelling. We don't need the guards to come rushing in here and find you like this."

"No, no, no," she said quickly. "No, definitely not."

"I'm going to begin," he announced. "Bite your lip if you must, or bury your head in the coverlets."

As he began spanking he let his smacks carry the message of discipline, but did not land them with the same force as he had at the waterfall. Falling into an easy rhythm, bouncing his hand across her curvaceous bottom, he felt her tension begin to slip away; her focus had shifted from the night's tumultuous events to his hand, and the sting she was feeling.

"Lizbett," he said softly, "have you discovered the pleasure that lies with the sweet nugget between your legs?"

"Larian, you ask me such a question?"

"Don't you recall, when we were younger, I would sometimes stroke you there?"

"Yes, I remember," she wriggled, her voice muffled as she buried her head in the sheets.

"Have you done this yourself? Stroked and caressed down there? Tell me."

"I have…sometimes…and I do feel things, but not that big thing that I've heard whispered about, the tingling explosion that is supposed to happen."

"I think now would be an excellent time to bring this into your life. Spread your legs for me."

"Oh, Sir," she whimpered.

"Do as I say, I promise you'll be so happy you did."

Tentatively she separated her legs, and when he gently rolled the silky robe up and over her glorious rump, he discovered flimsy pink underwear. It appeared delicate against her cheeks, and he could see the red hue courtesy of his spanking shining through the almost translucent fabric.

"I will not bare you," he said warmly, "but I am going to put my fingers against you, against that sweet, hungry nugget."

"It does feel hungry," she bleated. "That's the perfect word. It does want to be touched very much."

"And now it will be," he crooned slipping his hand against her.

The crotch of the thin undergarment was slick with her need, and pressing against the warm dampness he sighed with his own pleasure, relishing the promise of taking her for the first time. Shaking away the thought he moved his fingers to the small nub waiting for attention.

"Larian," she murmured, "oh, I need you to do that."

"I know, now sink into my lap and feel the pleasure. Focus on my fingers and how they touch you."

He began the ardent massage keeping a steady pressure, and guided by her moans he pressed harder, allowing his fingers to gain speed.

"Something…something is…is happening," she gasped.

69

"Yes, it is happening," he assured her. "Let it overwhelm you."

"Ooh, ooh, Larian…it's…"

"Bury your head," he said quickly, suddenly realizing she might not have the presence of mind to stifle her cries.

A moment later her bottom suddenly rose, her body grew taut, and with a soft, muffled howling she exploded into the joy.

CHAPTER TEN

They were stretched out on her bed, Lizbett having fallen into a deep sleep almost immediately after nestling in his arms. Larian knew she was beyond exhaustion, and the light spanking and her first climax had allowed her to sink into a much needed rest.

He was not so fortunate; his member was surging in his trousers, and he was in desperate need of his own release. Carefully extricating himself from her entwining limbs he moved quietly off the mattress and looked around for the hanging curtain Handerah had described. He spied it on the far wall, and moving across the expansive room he pushed it aside, finding a chamber with a large inviting bed covered in rich fabrics and large cushions.

Oil lamps were dimly burning, and moving forward he saw an open door on the opposite side of the bed; to his delight it was an anteroom, with a tub offering the latest innovation, a small wheel that could be turned to release water into a large tub.

The Verdanians are such clever people, always creating some new marvel.

He gazed at it longingly, but too tired to take a soak he stripped off, washed himself quickly, then retired to the waiting bed. As he disposed of the many pillows and slipped between the warm coverlets his hand wandered to his cock, stiff and aching for relief.

Closing his eyes his mind wandered into his future; his hoped for wedding night. Lizbett was laying naked before him, her skin glowing with the fire's flame, her legs widely spread in readiness, and her full, ripe breasts with their nipples stark and pointing to the heavens lay begging for his teasing tongue.

The vision alone was enough for his member to spew its cream, but dropping his hand away he refused himself, wanting to imagine more.

After taking several deep breaths he returned his fingers to their work, this time seeing his bride on her hands and knees, her deep violet eyes staring back at him over her shoulder, her bottom glowing red from the spanks of his hand, her trough glistening with its need. Placing his cock inside her soaked sex he pushed forward, gently battering, then slithered into her pure, silky cavern taking her as his own, driving forth and claiming her.

As the need to burst again fell upon him there was no holding back; his cock vacated with a mighty eruption. His essence short forth and began dribbling down his hand, and groaning between clenched teeth he vowed he would make her his bride.

"I will hasten your training, you will be mine," he muttered between short ragged breaths.

The Zanderonian's were known for their inherent ability to be strong and athletic; their warriors were legendary, and to be a Warrior Of The First Order was an elite title; it meant the man possessed tremendous skill, power and stamina.

Larian had ridden for three passages of the moons to reach Verdana, resting only when his horse required it. Even though he'd barely closed his eyes for the duration of his journey he had remained mentally and physically sharp. He'd been able to foil the dastardly plot against King Handerah, and taking to his horse again he'd carried Falayla to her home and captured a runaway conspirator.

But now he knew it was time to indulge in the other trait for which the Zanderonian warriors were famous; the ability to sleep as if in a coma. The state was called Zinyana, and it rejuvenated the body and mind, sinking the subject so deeply into sleep the heart slowed to half its rate; there was no dreaming and no movement.

It was the only time the warrior was vulnerable; he could not leap from his bed, his waking was measured, and he had to straighten his body slowly. Once rising from the state and having eaten, his prowess and strength were restored. Foregoing further rest he could do all that was required for several days before needing to sink into Zinyana again.

To enter Zinyana the warrior had to be assured he was safe, that he would not have to vault into action. In battle half the regiment would guard and fight, while the other half indulged in Zinyana, this way the warriors fighting were always at their peak, but there was another element to Zinyana that only the most talented of warriors could master; it was the ability to waken at a specific time, and it was a requirement as a Commander.

Picturing the pink-silver of the two moons Larian began the process. Each warrior had his own symbol to trigger the state of Zinyana, and the glowing globes that hung low and large in the night sky were his.

The mystical moons filled his soul as he sank into the mattress, his heavy weight causing the feathers to flatten. It was at this time that he set his waking hour, and he chose the time when the West sun was rising. The East sun was the first to lift over the horizon, the West sun appeared a short time later; the two suns dictated the habits of many.

As he crossed the threshold into unconsciousness the moons dissolved, and seeming to come from a far distance the whisper of Lizbett's voice floated around him.

"Sleep well my warrior."

Moments later he was adrift, weightless yet heavy, and his body and mind began the process of restoration.

Because Larian was slipping into Zinyana he'd been unaware that Lizbett had crept into his bed chamber. She had been woken by a strange grunting noise, and fearful that some loathsome creature had stolen into her chamber she had buried herself deeply under her coverlets. The frightening sound hadn't lasted very long, and when all was still and quiet she had pulled away her blankets and stared around the room.

Though she was relieved there was nothing to be seen the odd sound had left her shaken, and hoping Larian had taken himself to the chamber next to hers she had slipped from her bed and peeked through the curtain. She was greatly relieved to see him, and feeling better she was about to return to her bed when she recalled what she'd heard about the state of Zinyana.

If he's doing that, he won't know if I cuddle up next to him. I could spend all my sleeping hours against his body. That would be sheer heaven. Hmmm, but how do I know he's doing the Zinyana thing?

Creeping into the chamber she'd softly called his name, but he did not stir. Reaching the side of his bed she'd poked his shoulder, and received no response. Smiling happily she'd carefully pulled back the covers to join him, but when she did she saw his manhood; his hand was resting over it. Never having seen the sight before she gazed down, utterly captivated.

It looks so...lifeless...how can that thing possibly bring so much pleasure like everyone says? I know it's supposed to grow bigger but it certainly doesn't look like much.

Sighing heavily she'd climbed in next to him and pulled the covers over them both.

"Sleep well my warrior," she'd murmured, and curling next to him had fallen back asleep.

When the warrior lifts out of Zinyana it begins with a tingling in his fingers. As the tingle radiates up his arm the muscles stretch of their own accord, then his eyes begin to flutter open.

Lizbett had moved his arm and curled herself around it, and when Larian began his waking process something felt wrong. His right arm was tingling as it should, the muscles were reacting and his arm was beginning to stretch out, but his left arm was having difficulty.

He knew not to panic; there could be reasons why the waking was not proceeding as it should. He'd been very tired, and may not have had his arm long and flat as he was supposed to, but he was sure his body had been properly laid out. His fear was that the castle security had been compromised and someone had bound his arm to incapacitate him.

As he felt the tiny muscles in his eyelids come back to life he waited, controlling his anxiety until they were fully restored, then very slowly opened his eyes.

The chamber was the one in which he'd gone to sleep, there was no-one else there, but his arm felt as though there was a mighty weight upon it. Darting his eyes to the side, prepared to fling his right arm across his body to attack whatever he might find, he saw the familiar curly red hair.

Lizbett!

Sighing heavily he surrendered back to the process of waking, allowing each of his limbs to return to their full state, but thanks to Lizbett his left arm would not be as it should for a while.

I will spank you until your bottom matches the color of your hair. What a willful, disobedient girl you are, so much worse than I thought. Your father was right, you are impossible. I will tame you though, yes I will, and spanking isn't the only weapon I have at my disposal.

CHAPTER ELEVEN

Lizbett opened her eyes and stared around the room. She felt groggy, but the light beaming through the windows told her it was late and the suns were high in the sky. Yawning happily she smiled at how marvelous it had been to sleep next to the strong, protective body of her warrior, then shuddered deliciously when she recalled the previous night and the great pleasure he had shown her.

Mmmm, I must touch my fingers there again. Maybe I can do it for myself now, maybe he has released me.

Her arm was bent at the elbow, the back of her hand resting near her head, and she began to move it slowly downwards, but it unexpectedly caught. Turning her head she was shocked to discover her wrist had been bound with a thin rope, and that rope was secured to the bedpost.

"What is this?" she protested, and as she attempted to sit up she discovered she could not; her opposite wrist and both her ankles were also tethered. "Who has done this to me?" she wailed. "Show yourself. You must be a coward to tie a woman like this."

Movement across the room caught her eye, and she sighed in relief when she saw it was Larian.

"Thank goodness! Look, Larian, look what someone has done to me!"

She watched him ambling towards the bed and began squirming impatiently.

"Why are you moving so slowly? Please, Larian, please hurry and get me out of these ropes."

He stopped at the foot of the bed, and crossing his arms he glowered down at her.

"I tied you!" he declared.

"What? You? Why?"

"If you do not know then I must leave," he growled walking away.

"Wait? Where are you going? You can't leave me like this. I won't allow it. Why? Why did you do this? Tell me, I demand you tell me."

Ignoring her he continued to move away, but just as he was about to leave the chamber he turned around.

"Think about the question you asked me," he said sternly, then disappeared through the curtain.

"STOP! COME BACK HERE!"

Her voice was loud and shrill, and she groaned with great relief when he suddenly reappeared.

"Thank goodness! I should think so!"

He moved swiftly across the room, and only when he sat next to her did she notice what was in his hand.

"No, not the horse bit thing, no!"

"Screaming is not acceptable. I'm going to leave it right here," he said placing it next to her. "If you yell like that again it will go inside your mouth, but be warned, I've added a very distasteful potion and you won't like it."

"How long are you going to leave me here," she pleaded.

"I told you to think about the last question you asked, before you began screeching that is. When you have the answer to that question, then, and only then, will I consider releasing you."

Speechless, she watched him stand up and march away, then stared at the bit laying next to her. She wanted to wail at him, she wanted to yell and pound her fists on his chest, but she certainly didn't want that thing back between her teeth. Sighing heavily she closed her eyes and thought about his comment.

"I told you to think about the last question you asked."

Why? That was my question, why did you do this to me? He's punishing me for something, yes, he's punishing me. That's the answer. Wait, that's only part of the answer. Why is he punishing me? Ooh, because I snuck into his chamber and climbed into bed with him. Of course, but he was sleeping. What does it matter? If only I'd woken first I could have snuck away and he'd never have known. Oh well, at least I have the answer now.

"Larian, I know why," she called.

Silence.

"Larian!" she called again, a little louder.

"LARIAN!"

His body whistled through the curtain and zipped across the room so quickly she barely had time to catch her breath before he was placing the bit between her teeth.

"HUMPHH!"

"I warned you," he said sternly, standing up scowling down at her. "Does everyone jump when you yell? Did you expect me to come running because you think you have the answer? Foolish girl," he scolded. "You called once, that was enough. You will learn I will come when I'm ready to come, not because you yell for me. I was very clear, scream and the bit goes in your mouth. Now you will stay tied up even longer."

"Hmphf," she bleated, her eyes pleading up at him.

"Enough! Not another sound!"

Turning quickly he strode away, and as Lizbett saw the curtain flutter in his wake the first bitter taste of the potion on the hard rubber between her lips began to fill her mouth.

Oh, this is dreadful, what is it? Ooh, this is... but before she could finish her thought a small voice began chattering in her head.

Larian is a warrior, he is a Warrior Of The FIrst Order, he is a Commander. His will is iron, his promise is gold, his threats are real, his mind is as sharp as his sword. You have his love, but if you want him you have to realize he means what he says. If you want him you will have to obey him. If you want him you will have to be...a...a good girl, a really good girl.

The truth sent a ripple through her heart, then a chill down her spine, and closing her eyes his actions swam around her head. She recalled him lifting the nefarious traitor from behind the table and hurling him at her father's feet like a rag doll; his warm, protective hold as he'd taken her in his arms when he'd returned so late the night before; his kindness towards the humble village maiden. Hot tears began to brim behind her eyes.

But I am not good, I've never been good. I may be a Princess, but I've never been good, and I'm certainly not good enough for you, Larian. You have become a warrior of the highest order, but I have become nothing...just older.

Her body began to sink into the mattress as the wetness dribbled from the sides of her eyes.

Larian had not gone anywhere; he was watching from a small gap in the curtain. When he heard the sigh he was hopeful, and when she began to softly moan, and then sob, he prayed it signaled what he believed it did.

Moving quietly across the room he sat beside her, and when her eyes opened and she stared up at him he saw vulnerability and understanding flowing with her tears. Reaching behind her head he unbuckled the bit and gently removed it.

"Larian," she whispered, "I know the why, but I know so much more."

"I'm listening," he said softly.

"The why is because I...I...ignored your wishes and crept into your bed last night. I know about Zinyana, and that you probably wouldn't wake, and you didn't, but that was so wrong and I'm sorry, and that's why you tied me up."

"Yes, that is the why. What else do you know?"

"I know that...that...I am not good. I have never been good, and you were right when you said I disobey just because I can. I'm not a good girl, I'm not good at all, not good enough for you," she exclaimed, and with a heaving sigh she broke into sobs.

"The dawn of understanding. It is such a moment to behold," he murmured, and reaching across her body, with one pull of the rope, all her limbs were simultaneously released.

"Larian? What are you saying?" she blubbered not even caring that she was free.

"Come here," he crooned pulling her into his body. "Have faith, sweet Lizbett. You will travel with me to my residence, and I will help you free the good girl who lives inside you."

"I don't know how," she moaned.

"I think perhaps you do," he smiled.

"Can I say something?"

"You asked for permission. See, we are making progress already. Yes, you may say anything you wish, as long as it isn't unkind."

She pressed even closer against him, curling her head into his shoulder.

"I feel so amazing when your arms are around me. It's as if nothing can harm me. If feel so safe. I always want them to hold me like this."

Closing his eyes Larian inhaled her sweet scent, relishing her soft, yielding body as it dissolved into his.

"I shall always be your strength and your protector," he whispered. "I promise, and you know I always keep my promises."

He rocked her for a short time, then she lifted her head and gazed up at him.

"How long will this awful taste be in my mouth?"

"For a while," he nodded, "like the sting of my hand. It remains to remind you of your crime; it helps you the next time you might want to be naughty."

"Oh, a while?"

"Yes, a while, but speaking of your lovely mouth, I believe we both need to have our morning meal."

"The servants will have left a large tray outside my door," she replied. "Can you bring it in, please? I will wash my face and meet you at the table by the window."

"I must be quick. I have to seek out the King and hear what information was uncovered."

"I'm sure there will be a great deal," she frowned. "I need a long soak before I venture out."

"Then I will eat with you, and leave you to your girly ways," he smiled, and kissing her forehead he slowly moved her off his lap and headed for the curtain.

Entering her bed chamber he opened the door to the foyer and found exactly what she had described; a large tray covered in plates offering a variety of food. Carrying it across to the table by the window, he pulled on his long pants and sat down to eat. He was ravenous and his arm was still lagging; he'd need another hour of Zinyana to fully restore the blood that was not circulating properly.

You are a very naughty girl, Lizbett, but this morning we have crossed a barrier. You have many sore bottoms in your future, and many more lessons, but you will get there.

CHAPTER TWELVE

A fter sharing breakfast overlooking the gardens with the golden mountains gleaming in the distance, it was time for Larian to leave for his audience with the King. Standing up he took her hand, pulled her into his chest, and hugged her warmly.

"Larian," she murmured, "I love being in your arms."

Moving his lips to her neck he kissed her languidly, then straightening up he traced her face with his fingertips.

"I must go, sweet Princess, but soon we will be on our way to my home. Pack only what you need, just one bag."

"One bag? I'll try," she muttered trying to think of the largest bag she had.

"I have to go. After I meet with your father I must return to my bed chamber and enter Zinyana again to restore arm. I'll come back here to fetch you when the East sun is halfway set"

"I'll be ready," she promised.

Moving quickly to the main foyer of the King's apartments he was told that the monarch was in his personal suite of rooms surrounded by heavy security; Larian took that to mean the King believed a threat still existed.

As he approached the door to the King's private apartment the same routine was applied as it had been the night before; he was stopped and his visit checked before he was allowed entry.

"I'm sorry you were halted, Larian," the King apologized. "My personal retinue is extremely loyal and determined that no harm shall come to me."

"No apology is necessary. I am pleased they are so diligent."

"Larian, is your arm injured? It is hanging in a most peculiar fashion."

"Sire, I will be frank. I wish to have no secrets; this is the fault of your daughter."

"Lizbett? How could she possibly hurt your arm?"

"I was in the state of Zinyana in the bed chamber next to hers. She was willful, as well you know she can be, and against my wishes she crept in and laid next to me. Because of the weight of her body on my arm it could not reawaken properly. I now must sleep for a short time and rise again."

"I'm sorry, Larian, that daughter of mine is impossible," the King sighed. "I do hope you possess the patience to deal with her."

"I believe I do, Sire. I took some steps to discipline her and I believe I made my point. Rest assured I will continue to make it clear such naughtiness will not be tolerated."

"I'm glad you did," the King said solemnly, "you must do as you see fit. It is on my shoulders that she is such a difficult young woman."

"My only wish is to see her happy and content," Larian said warmly. "A woman is not happy if she is disobedient and willful, at least, this is the belief of the Zanderonians."

"I share your belief. I make sure my wife knows I am King, believe me, but as much as I am enjoying this conversation we must speak of more serious matters."

"Yes, what news was uncovered? I am eager to hear."

"As we feared there were others involved in the attempted seizure of the throne. Only a handful, but they are still at large. You must remain on high alert as you travel back to your residence."

"Ah, this is good information, thank you."

"Take note, Larian, there are four men, all nobles, three share the black hair and orange eyes of their heritage so they will be easy to uncover. The fourth is a distant relative and has reddish hair and blue eyes, and if he is disguised as a villager or a merchant he will be more difficult to spot. We think they're traveling together which is helpful, but they stole horses so they may be far away by now."

"I hope they are. If they are gone they don't pose a threat," Larian remarked.

"I do not share your view. If they are gone they can regroup, join others and launch a different type of attack. I shall not rest, Larian, until they are found."

"Ah, yes, Sire, I understand. It is good Lizbett will be away from here. I imagine such men might see her as your weakness."

"They would be right," Handerah sighed, "and I would be very worried about your journey, but knowing there is the compartment in which she can hide, and that she will be escorted by you and the warriors of Zanderone fills me with confidence."

"My men will need only two hours of Zinyana and then they will be ready to travel."

"It's amazing that you can do that," Handerah declared. "It is truly remarkable and such a blessing."

"It is, Sire, but when we sleep, young women like Lizbett can be very naughty."

Handerah laughed out loud.

"It is good to joke when such serious matters surround us," he chuckled.

"It is important," Larian said. "Laughter and humor help us deal with the serious matters in life."

"Indeed," Handerah nodded, "and you have brightened my day."

"Thank you, Sire, I'm glad of it. Now I must return to my chambers for an undisturbed, short sleep. Lizbett is packing, but I have told her only one bag."

"That will be quite the challenge," the King said raising his eyebrows.

"If I am still in sleep when the carriage and men arrive, would you please allow them a secure apartment where they may have their own time to sink into Zinyana and restore themselves? They will need sustenance upon waking, this is part of the process."

"I shall give the orders immediately. The horses will be seen to and new ones provided."

"Ah, I'm so pleased you mentioned the horses. I believe it would be beneficial for Lizbett to have her horse, Scarlet, come with her. I fully intend that she learn to ride in the manner she should, and Scarlet must also be trained to accept this."

"I will see the mare is ready, though it is a long trek for her."

"We will not be racing, Sire, and from what I saw the mare is not given the exercise she needs. I suspect she will enjoy the journey, and as you are aware we are taught much about horses and how to care for them."

"Yes, of course you are. My mind is filled with too many things, and you're right, Lizbett is very attached to her horse. She will take comfort in having her there."

"Thank you, Sire, and if I may?"

"Yes?"

"I know you are very worried, but I believe these other schemers will be quickly captured. The head has been cut off the snake. It may wriggle, but its fangs are gone. Please, Sire, please get some rest and good food. Your Kingdom is safe."

Handerah stared at the muscled young warrior; his wisdom was far greater than his youth would suggest.

"Farris was my friend, my confidant, my advisor. His betrayal has distressed me greatly," the King confessed as a heavy frown creased his brow.

"A man is trustworthy only until he is not," Larian said quietly. "You must find someone new, but until that person surfaces you can always contact me, and your wife will soon be at your side."

The King stepped forward and squeezed his arm, a gesture of great fondness.

"The summer your Prince sent you to my stable, is the summer that assured the future of this Kingdom. I will take your wise words to heart."

Bathed in the King's warm approval Larian bowed his head, and overcome by the high praise he murmured a humble thank you, then backing up three steps he turned and left the chamber.

As he headed down the long passageway, his arm hanging uncomfortably at his side, his mind was swirling.

He wanted to stay and help the King, he wanted to track down the remaining traitors, and he knew he could find them. An excellent hunter, Larian could cajole, he could threaten, he could size men up and know if they were hiding something…or someone.

Though Lizbett needed to be taken to safety, the security at the castle was tight, it would be almost impossible to gain access to her, but he also wanted her at his new home, he wanted to train her, to help her, to make her happy.

The words of the Prince he served began echoing through the corridors of his mind. It was as he was about to mount his horse to leave for Verdana that the Prince had taken him aside to give him some parting advice.

There will come a time, Larian, when you will be pulled in different directions. A man such as yourself will be needed, and sought after, and with your heart you will want to serve all who ask. You must remember that though you are mighty, you are only one. When you find yourself torn select the most important task and give that the attention. If you split yourself, those you wish to help will end up suffering for it, as will you.

Reaching his chamber, the advice in the forefront of his mind, he closed and bolted the door, then noticed a tray of tempting looking food had been laid on his table.

Excellent. I'll need that when I wake, and I shall pack some for the journey.

Laying himself upon the bed he closed his eyes, picturing the silver-pink moons, and taking long deep breaths he pondered his Prince's sage words.

Lizbett. Her safety comes first.

The deep sleep began to take hold.

An opportunity to help the King will present itself.

The precognitive thought washed through him; it happened sometimes, a knowingness, a tiny peek into the future. It was always vague but it was always proven accurate, and he knew it would not have come upon him had he not made the right decision. At peace, he descended in the heavy state of Zinyana, his final thought was waking when the sun had moved a slight distance across the sky.

In her apartment Lizbett was having an impossible time fitting all she needed into just one bag. Her servant was doing her best to help, but the Princess was becoming more and more frustrated.

"I must have at least three gowns," Lizbett wailed. "I can barely fit one, and they will become wrinkled if they're pushed in too tightly."

"Could we take the wrapping off them?" the servant suggested.

"No! I will not have anything soil them. You know how I feel about any marks on my clothes. They must look perfect, even my petticoats and underthings must keep their wrapping. I will not have any of my clothing become blemished."

"Perhaps you can send for more when you reach, uh, wherever it is you're going."

"This will not work! I must have at least three bags! One for my finer dresses, one for my riding clothes and casual wear, and one for my undergarments and shoes and lotions and such."

"Do you wish me to bring you two more bags, Princess?"

"Yes. He'll just have to understand women need more than men. I've had enough of this. Pack three bags as I've described. I'm going to the stables to ride Scarlet."

As she flounced out the door, a quadrant of guards gathered around her and hurried alongside.

"Princess, where are we headed? We're instructed to advise the King of your whereabouts at all times."

"The stables, to see my mare," she announced.

One of the guards split off to hurry to the King's apartments with the information, while the remaining three shared a panicked look.

"I wouldn't worry," she said blithely. "Think about it; if there are any traitors left they won't be on the castle grounds, they'd have to be complete idiots."

Unconvinced, the guards kept their eyes darting around them as they headed down the many hallways and out into the courtyard.

CHAPTER THIRTEEN

Larian had risen from his short sleep, found his arm had completely recovered, and was enjoying the food that had been left when an urgent banging sounded on his door.

"I'm glad I'm awake," he muttered as he hurried to answer it.

Unbolting the latch he discovered a young stable boy; the lad appeared very agitated and Larian immediately thought something had happened to Thunder, his prized horse.

"Sir, I'm so sorry to pound upon your door but Tholl send me to find you, it's about the Princess."

"What's happened?" Larian asked feeling his heart skip.

"She's insisting on taking a ride on Scarlet and-"

"I understand," Larian interrupted, and darting past him began running down the passageway. The young boy stood stunned as he watched Larian gather speed; the warrior was sprinting faster than he'd ever seen anyone run before.

Larian reached the stable yard just in time to see Lizbett trying to pull Scarlet's reins from Tholl's grip. The guards were standing by ready to mount up and accompany her should she win the battle, and as Larian stopped and scanned the scene it was obvious Lizbett had caused a complete ruckus.

Though Scarlet was bridled there was no saddle on her back, and the mare was jigging up and down, spooked by the histrionics of her owner; Tholl's face was red and furrowed, and while the guard's horses were saddled, standing quietly, the guards themselves looked extremely anxious. To complete the chaotic picture the stable lads were cowering in the background, looking terrified of everyone and everything that was happening.

"It is not safe," Larian heard Tholl declare as she continued to yank on the reins.

"Of course it is," she barked. "I have the guards to protect me, and those traitors won't be anywhere near the castle grounds. If they are we'll catch them. There's nothing I'd like better."

"No, Princess, your father would be most upset if I allowed you to take your horse out, even with the guards."

"Give me the reins," she bellowed.

"ENOUGH!"

Larian's deep voice boomed through the stable courtyard and everyone froze; even Scarlet stopped her jigging, spinning her head around and looking in Larian's direction.

"You may unsaddle your mounts," he said lowering his voice and speaking calmly to the guards. "Tholl, did you receive orders to prepare Scarlet for travel?"

"I did, and I was doing so when-"

"When I arrived to take her for one last ride," Scarlet interrupted.

"She does not need to be ridden, she needs to be prepared for her journey, and you do not need to be riding off anywhere," Larian said firmly, then stepping forward he opened his palm and extended it towards Lizbett. "Hand me the reins."

Her violet eyes stared back at him and he saw the challenge, but it was fleeting, and dropping her head she handed them over.

"Please wait for me in your chambers. I'll be there momentarily."

Without a word she hurried away, and the stable lads rushed forward to take the horses from the guards so they would be able to follow her and continue their protection.

"Larian, thank goodness," Tholl sighed.

"Such a handful," Larian remarked, "I must get her back to my residence. Things will be much easier for us there. I wish the carriage and my men would arrive. They should be here by now."

"I have checked the mare for the journey. She seems fine. Her feet were just trimmed, she's eaten well today. She has too much energy for the amount of riding the Princess does, but..."

"But the Princess is the only one permitted to ride her."

"Yes," Tholl replied sighing again.

"I think the mare will thoroughly enjoy the long excursion," Larian remarked.

"She will, I'm sure of it," Tholl agreed.

"You know I will be taking fresh carriage horses from here?" Larian asked.

"Yes, they're ready to go, they're excellent. I trained them myself," Tholl said proudly.

"Then I shall not worry," Larian smiled. "I want to start the journey in the carriage with the Princess so Thunder should be tethered behind it, but with his saddle on in case of any trouble."

"I'll see it," Tholl promised.

"My men's horses should be traded as well. I hesitate only because they are so well trained, and we don't know what we might face on the journey back to my home."

"How many men do you have?"

"Six."

"The King said to give you whatever you need, so I will provide you with the six that will see you home safely, come battle or peace," Tholl offered.

"Excellent. Then it is settled. Now, do you have a small, thin riding stick?"

"Yes, here you are," Tholl smiled handing Larian a dark brown, leather-wrapped, narrow rod.

"This will do nicely, thank you."

"I don't have to ask what that's for."

"Sometimes a point must be made," Larian winked.

Scarlet, who was still nervously moving her feet, suddenly let out a snort as if concurring with the two men.

"Scarlet," Larian said softly, gently stroking her neck, "you must not worry, your life is about to become far more tolerable."

His assured, even voice and tender caress began to calm her, and when she let out a sigh and dropped her head, Tholl smiled broadly.

"You have the touch, Larian," he nodded. "You always did."

"Thank you for everything, Tholl, and most especially for sending the stable boy to find me. You did the right thing."

"I'm not sure the Princess will see it that way," he grimaced.

"The Princess will see as I wish her to," Larian declared, "and is that a carriage I hear?"

The sound of approaching whinnies and the drawbridge being lowered caused both men to step out of the stable yard and look across the courtyard. The large carriage surrounded by the six men wearing the uniforms of the Zanderone warrior moved slowly across the bridge, then continued forward and came to a stop.

"Thank you, again, Tholl," Larian said quickly, and running forward enthusiastically greeted his men.

"We were held up, Commander, the marauders."

It was Zoltaire, the leader of the group and Larian's righthand man who offered the news.

"Did you pull your sword?"

"No, Sir, I remembered your advice; pull your sword and you ask to fight. We talked, I assured them they would suffer greatly if they attempted to steal from us, and after we exchanged words for a while they saw the better choice and left us in peace."

"Well done, Zoltaire. This shall not go unnoticed."

"I believe a woman is attempting to get your attention," Zoltaire smiled.

Turning around Larian saw Delina approaching, and knew she had come to show his warriors where they could rest and eat.

"Thank you for coming down, Delina," he said warmly. "Zoltaire, Delina will show you to chambers where you can safely enter Zinyana. We will leave when the West sun sets. It is better we move out in the shadow of darkness. Much has happened here, but I will tell you about that later."

"Yes, Commander."

"The stable master is Tholl. He is the man who taught me much when I was here in my youth; he will provide you with fresh horses, both to ride and for the carriage."

"Excellent. Thank you, Commander. We will sleep and eat, and be ready."

Knowing his men were in capable hands, Larian hurried to Lizbett's apartment and this time the guards did not stop him, but bowed their heads and opened the door as he approached.

Firmly gripping the riding stick he moved through the foyer, and without knocking strode into Lizbett's bed chamber. She was standing by the windows, staring out at the mountains in the distance, and when she heard the door close she spun around.

"Larian, is everything all right? You took so long. I thought you were right behind me."

"I had matters to discuss with Tholl, then my men arrived," Larian replied. "Is there anything you'd like to say?"

"Only that I should have been able to take Scarlet out for a short ride," she declared. "I'm very upset with Tholl for refusing to cooperate. I hope you put him in his place. The nerve of that man!"

Larian broke into a large smile.

"That was very good, Lizbett. Were I not trained in the wily ways of women I might not have seen through it."

"I don't know what you mean," she retorted, but even as she spoke she felt the betrayal of the red blush as it crossed her face.

"Your crimson cheeks betray you," he said pointedly.

"I'm just excited about leaving!"

"Is your servant here?"

"Uh, no, she finished her work and has left to pack me some food for the journey. Why? Do you need to see her?"

"You know why, you also know you were totally in the wrong, and it is time to stop this foolish ruse and admit what a naughty girl you've been."

He watched her struggle as the conflict raged inside her; his assessment was right.

The moment his voice had commanded attention when he'd arrived at the stable, Lizbett had known she was in trouble. Not only had Larian caught her fighting with one of his great teachers, she knew she was totally in the wrong and Tholl's reasoning was sound.

It wasn't the safest of times to be out on her horse, even with the guards, and she also knew the carriage was due to arrive and she shouldn't be leaving anyway. She wasn't even sure why she had thrown her tantrum and caused a scene; it was just something she'd felt compelled to do.

Now Larian was standing in front of her and had called her bluff, and still she was playing the game, acting the innocent, trying to distract him from her guilt. It was a game at which she excelled, but Larian wasn't like everybody else; Larian could see right through her.

"Yes, all right," she murmured. "I surrender. I was wrong, and just now I tried to divert attention from the scene I caused."

"What do you think I should do about that?"

"Uh, well, since I've just admitted my wrongdoing, probably nothing," she suggested, knowing full well it was a foolish response.

"Still you try? You are relentless. It's a good trait to have, but sometimes it can get you into even more trouble. I'll give you one more chance. What do you think I should do about it?"

"You are so hard," she groaned.

"I'm waiting."

"Since I am about to sit in a carriage for some time, I would think something other than spanking," she said quietly.

"Just the opposite," he declared. "I think sitting on a sore bottom is exactly what you need. Come over here and bend across your bed."

"Sir?" she bleated.

"Yes, I am your Sir, and I'm pleased you addressed me as such. Quickly, there are things I must see to while my men are sleeping."

As she shuffled across the room she spied the riding stick in his hand; her pulse quickened; it looked nasty.

"You're going to use that?" she whimpered.

"I most certainly am," he said firmly.

She paused for just a moment, staring at it, and he was happy she did; the fear of the thing rolling through her veins would only add to the anticipation, and anticipation was in itself a key element of any punishment.

Laying herself over the edge of the mattress, she cringed as her dress and the underlying petticoats were placed on her back, exposing her again in her thin, silky underwear.

"This will hurt," he warned. "Face into the bed."

She felt the stick lay lightly across the center of her cheeks; clenching her teeth she waited for the first stroke and it was a short wait; Larian dispatched the stick with a zinging swish.

Her leg kicked out, not as a conscious protest but an involuntary response, and as the burning mark radiated through her bottom she groaned into the bed.

Wasting no time he delivered the second and third, laying them close to each other, and seeing the angry red lines through the fine fabric he knew they were smarting keenly.

"Lizbett, you knew what you were doing was absolutely wrong, didn't you?"

"Yes, Sir, I did."

"Tell me why you did it."

"I'm honestly not sure, Sir, but I think it might have been the bags."

"The bags? What bags?"

"I became extremely frustrated and angry about the bags, I mean, being allowed only one. It was impossible, so I sent my servant to fetch two more even though I knew you would not allow them."

"Ah, so your little scene at the stable was a rebellious act; you were angry about one thing, so you chose another to voice your discontent."

"I, uh, yes, Sir, I think so."

"You can't always have things the way you want them, Lizbett. I understand this is new for you, but do you see where your moment of rebellion has landed? Directly across the seat of your bottom."

"Yes, Sir, and it hurts very much."

"You will not need gowns or fine clothes, and you will receive one more stroke for not following my instructions about the bag, then I will leave you. I will return when the West sun is about to set."

"Sir?" she whimpered.

"Yes?"

"Thank you for making arrangements to bring Scarlet."

"Do you think that will get you out of the last stroke?"

"No, Sir, I just wanted to say it."

"Is it possible you're really saying, thank you for punishing me? I deserve it and I want it?"

She paused, then moaned into the mattress.

How does he know these things?

He is a Zanderonian warrior, it has been said they understand women, and they are the only men who do.

"Yes, Sir," she whispered.

"Then let me hear it. It will please me, and it will help you."

"Thank you for punishing me, Sir, I deserve it, and…and…"

"Yes, go on."

"And I want it."

The fourth stroke sliced through the air, kissing her skin with fire, but before she had time to feel the depth of the stinging flame he had swept her up and was holding her tenderly.

"Dearest Lizbett, I must discipline you because I love you, because I want you to be happy and at peace. Any time you feel anger towards me because I punish you, please remember that."

Surrendering into his arms she let out a long breath.

"Yes, Sir, I will, and I love you back, so very much."

He held her until he knew she was feeling whole again, then gently kissing her he took his leave. He did have matters that needed his attention, and one of them was standing at attention in his pants.

CHAPTER FOURTEEN

The suns had set, and after tearfully hugging her father goodbye Lizbett donned a hooded cloak and hurried across the courtyard. Waiting for her at the door of the carriage Larian helped her inside then climbed in after her. Being an outstanding horseman, Zoltaire had been chosen to lead Scarlet as he rode his own horse until the mare settled down, then she would be attached to the carriage next to Thunder.

Flanked either side by the warriors the carriage rolled slowly out of the castle grounds, over the drawbridge and on to the road. The moons would be high in the sky when they crossed through the wall that surrounded Verdana, and then they would be in open country. They would be safe until the following day when they would enter the barren land where the marauders lived.

Larian wanted to travel the perilous part of the journey during the daylight hours. If the marauders did attempt to stop them Larian would see them coming; it would offer him and his warriors time to prepare, giving them the advantage. The barren land was flat and dry, there were no boulders the marauders could hide behind, only a few shrubs, so there was no fear of an ambush.

Larian wasn't concerned about them per se; they weren't a threat. They were weak fighters and even if significantly outnumbered the warriors would easily cut them down, but he didn't want Lizbett to see battle; it was bloody and ugly. He also didn't want them to see her; she would be the only reason they might risk a fight.

As they reached the outskirts of the kingdom, Lizbett curled up against him and nestled her head into his shoulder.

"Won't we stop at all until we reach your house?"

"Yes, Lizbett, of course," he replied pulling down the shades to block anyone peering inside. "The horses need the rest, and you will too. We will travel until we pass the barren land, then we will be guests of an elderly uncle of mine. He was once a fierce warrior and he is a legend in our Kingdom."

"Why doesn't he still live there?"

"He could, and he is always welcome, but when his days serving the realm came to an end, the Prince gifted him a beautiful home atop a knoll, with much land and many animals. It has a forest in which he can hunt, a lake in which he can fish and swim, and he is living his life in peace and harmony with the woman he married as a young warrior. He has grown children and they have many children, and there is always family coming and going."

"It sounds wonderful. What a happy way to live out your life," Lizbett sighed.

"He suffered greatly for it," Larian remarked.

He fell quiet, and Lizbett saw there were painful stories about his uncle Larian held dear, and close to his heart.

"My bottom is so sore," she complained thinking she should change the subject.

"I'm glad. What a naughty girl you were. I hope you're ashamed of yourself, carrying on like such a spoiled child."

"I didn't tell it was sore so you scold me again," she pouted. "I told you so you would hug me as you did after you whipped me."

"There is a time for tenderness, a time for punishment, and a time for truth. You just heard the truth."

"Oh, Larian, you can be so hard."

"You said that earlier."

"You were hard then as well!"

"I will be hard whenever necessary," he said firmly, then suddenly gripping her hair he yanked it back and gazed his aqua eyes into hers. "And whenever I want to kiss you, I will do that too."

His warrior's mouth pressed on hers, then moved slowly, gently kissing, then artfully he slipped both his lips over her lower one and began to suck. His clutching hand prevented any movement, and when his other hand began to fondle her breasts she let out a cry of surprise, then a moan of need, then slowly releasing her lips he brought his mouth to her ear.

"That is one way I will kiss you, and I will do so whenever I choose. Just as I will caress these beautiful breasts when I choose, or touch your womanliness on the outside of her underwear when I choose, and the inside too, when we reach my house. I will rub your nugget when I choose, I will suckle your nipples when I choose, and pinch them," he said, quickly tweaking her nipples with the tips of his fingers.

"Ouch..ooh...but it feels so good," she moaned, "you are making me weak."

"I know, and as I teach you the ways of your body you will grow much weaker, and that is how you must be. That is where your happiness lies, and also your strength."

His hand was roaming over her stomach, moving lower, and she separated her legs, urgently pulling up the folds of fabric.

"Please, Sir, please rub me again as you did last night?"

"You call me Sir because you feel my authority when I have your hair clutched as I do, you call me Sir because you feel the power of my hand roaming across your body and you know it will possess you. Isn't that right, Lizbett?"

"Yes, Sir," she groaned. "Please, please touch me there again."

"You ask so sweetly and so I will, but only for a moment," he said softly, and moving his hand between her legs he whispered his fingers across the damp, thin gusset of her underwear.

"Ooh, more, please, more."

"No, no more," he replied pushing her hands from her dress so it would fall back around her legs. "Perhaps when we stop for our rest I will rub you and bring on that tingling moment, but only if you're a very good girl."

"But, Sir, I need it now, I really do. I feel hungry down there."

"You must remain hungry," he said firmly. "It is a good way for you to be."

"But why?" she bleated.

"It is all part of your learning," he said tenderly. "Now pay attention. In a moment I am going to release your hair, and you are going to do something for me."

"Anything you ask, Sir, anything."

"You saw my manliness when you crept into my bed, didn't you?"

A hot flush moved across her face, but she couldn't drop her head because her hair was coiled around his fingers and he was holding her tightly, so she lowered her eyelids.

"No, look at me," he ordered giving her hair a tug.

"Oh, Sir, I'm…I'm…"

"Embarrassed? You needn't be embarrassed. Tell me, what did you think?"

"I…uh…didn't know what to think, not at first," she stammered.

"And then?"

"And then I thought it looked soft, and kind of…sorry to say this, but…uh…weak."

"At that time it was, but now, now it is hard and strong, and when I release your hair you are to place your hand there."

"Sir?" she gasped.

"You will feel it through my clothes, then you will unfasten the patch that lays across the front of my trousers and you will pull it out."

"Oh, Sir, I'm not sure I can," she protested staring up at him.

"Of course you can, it won't bite," he smiled.

"I don't know why I feel so strange about it."

"You will do as I ask, or must I spank you again?"

"No, please, my bottom is so sore."

"Then you will obey me, yes?"

"Yes, I will obey you," she breathed.

He kissed her again, tenderly consuming her mouth before traveling to her neck and lightly nibbling, then rested his lips at her ear.

"Are you ready?"

"Yes, Sir."

He released her, and cautiously she looked down at his crotch. Tentatively she moved her hand to rest on the patch of fabric that was fastened at the waist by wooden buttons.

"It is so big and so hard," she breathed.

"Open the flap."

Her nimble fingers were trembling, but she managed to unfasten the thick buttons, and peeling back the swatch of fabric she stared at his bulging manhood.

"It is nothing like what I saw."

"Take hold of it," he said firmly. "There's nothing to be concerned about."

Carefully wrapping her fingers around its girth she continued to stare, and her trepidation slipped into curiosity.

"Move your hand up and down, rub it, massage it," he said, the tone of his voice deepening.

"Does it bring you pleasure, Sir, the way your fingers rubbing my nugget gives me pleasure? she asked as she carefully began to stroke.

"Yes, exactly the same," he growled, "don't stop."

"It is so...powerful...so...hard and big."

"On our wedding night I will slide it inside you, and pump you until you have that magical moment you had last night."

"On our wedding night?" she said softly, her violet eyes sparkling up at him.

"Yes, Lizbett. I have decided you are to be my wife."

"Larian," she breathed.

"That is very good, Lizbett, keep rubbing just like that."

"But, Larian…"

"You wish to say something?"

"All those other men who came to court me, they all asked me, begged me even, to be their wife. You just decided and so it is? Don't you want to ask me?"

"I am a Warrior Of The First Order. You have loved me since our youth, as I have loved you. Do you think I should have doubt?"

"No, it's just…"

"Lizbett, I am not like other men. I am not weak, or frail, and I don't ask a question when I already know the answer, not unless I want to catch someone in a lie. You are deliriously happy right now because you are to be my wife, you know our future is before us, and rather than question my methods perhaps you should be thanking me for choosing you."

"Oh, Larian, you spin my head and heart."

"I know, and that's how it should be, not the other way around, but why have you stopped rubbing? This is the perfect way to celebrate our engagement."

"It is, oh, it is," she sighed.

"You will rub it until it erupts. When it does I will groan, and then you will wipe away the mess, and I will be very pleased with you."

"I have nothing to wipe it with," she frowned.

"Yes, you do, your petticoats. I want you to wipe me clean with your petticoats. This way you will have my essence under your dress for half of our journey, and it will be our special secret."

"It will," she smiled. "It's a strange secret, but as I think about it, I like it."

"You'll have to wash it off when we reach my uncle's house, but this is a service you will do because you are mine now, and you wish to please me."

"Sir," she breathed, "you are right, you are different, so different, and you make me feel different."

"Be a good girl and rub, rub vigorously and make me happy."

"Yes, Sir, thank you for teaching me."

"This is just the beginning," he sighed surrendering to the pleasure of her fingers. "Just the very beginning."

Though slightly bewildered Lizbett was overjoyed; his offer of marriage wasn't like an offer at all. The others had brought her gifts, expensive gifts, and flowers and cakes, but none of them had made her feel as Larian did, as Larian was making her feel right at that moment, and that feeling was growing all the time. His announcement that he'd decided she would be his wife had made her feel the flippity flip, and as his member began to ooze tiny drops, and his breath grew short and rapid, the flippity flip began flipping even more.

"Yes, Lizbett, good girl, harder, harder, yes, good girl."

Fascinated, her eyes could not leave his cock, but the flippity flip had left her feeling oddly weak and she leaned against his chest for support; his heart was profoundly beating, so much so it almost frightened her, then unexpectedly it began to jerk.

The groan he'd promised was deep and long as his hot cream dribbled down her fingers. He was panting, and it was shriveling into the soft thing she'd seen resting under his hand, then he let out a heavy sigh and it was over. Quickly pulling up her dress she held the middle petticoat and wiped up the mess, then stared down at it.

"This is the most extraordinary thing," she declared.

"What is?" he panted.

"I just wiped your…stuff…all over my petticoat."

"Yes, you did," he sighed.

"Did you just cast a spell on me?"

"Yes, wife to be, I did."

"Thank goodness, because otherwise I'd think there was something very wrong with me," she frowned staring down at the wet stain on the pristine silk.

"Put me away and button the flap," he said softly, "then come and curl into me."

Laying his flaccid cock on its side, she pushed the edges of the flap back into the sides of the opening setting it into place, then fastened the buttons.

"You just did something very important," he whispered.

"Rubbing you like that? Is that what you mean?"

"That's part of it, but there was a bigger part. Can you guess what that was?"

She paused, burrowing more closely against his body, then a small smile crossed her lips.

"I know," she murmured.

"Tell me."

"I obeyed you without question or protest."

"Yes, Princess, you did, and I'm very proud of you. Now I must drift for a moment, and you should rest as well. Soon we will be at the barren land, and then we must be awake and alert."

"Yes, Larian," she sighed, and though there was still a restless yearning between her legs she curled into him and closed her eyes.

CHAPTER FIFTEEN

The miles ticked by, the moons glided across the sky, and the East sun began to shine its brilliance upon the land; Lizbett woke up and stared out at the full, rich landscape. This was the furthest she'd ventured outside Verdana and the foliage was decidedly different.

Orange and red trees hung with abundant flowers, and her sensitive nose smelled the myriad fragrances. Larian had been awake for some time, and had lifted the shades so she could see the view as soon as she stirred from sleep.

"It's so beautiful," she murmured, "and it smells tangy and sweet at the same time."

"No doubt you can appreciate the aromas better than most," he smiled, "but even I can smell the citrus flavors that linger in the air."

"I see fruits hanging, some of them I recognize but others I don't."

"When we reach my uncle's home you will enjoy them. He has many of these trees, and an abundance of their fruit, especially in this season."

"I'm so excited," she smiled, "I'm really enjoying this whole thing. I thought it would be more difficult to travel so far in this carriage, but it's not."

"We traveled quickly in the night," he remarked. "The roads were empty, and the horses enjoyed the brisk night air. There were stretches when they were galloping."

"Did you check on Scarlet? I'm worried about her."

"Yes, of course, we won't let anything happen to Scarlet. She is having a wonderful time, and still has energy. We thought she'd be ready to jog next to Thunder by now, but her enthusiasm is boundless."

"Where are we? Are we nearing the barren land?"

"Yes, it's not far. There's a small village where we will stop and take a break. You can stretch your legs and freshen up at the inn, we can have a quick meal, the horses can eat and drink, and then we will head forward into the only perilous part of the journey."

"Do you think we'll have trouble?"

"I don't. The marauders intercepted the carriage on the way to Verdana, and even stuffed with hampers of food my men were able to convince them to leave. They are not warriors, they are scavengers, and they do not wish to battle, especially not those who are superior. I'm surprised they even approached the carriage. They may have been curious, or even hoping some scraps would be thrown their way."

"So if they did attack us, you could deal with them?"

"I could deal with them by myself and step away with not a scratch. With all six of my men, they wouldn't even have time to lift their weapons."

"Oh, then, I'm not worried anymore," she smiled. "Can we stop and pick some fruit?"

"No, we must keep going, but the village is close."

"How are you this morning, Larian? Did you drift easily?" she giggled.

"I did, very easily," he replied. "I have a great deal of energy right now."

"You don't feel like this when you ride?"

"No. Sitting inside a carriage is not something I normally do, Princess," he said with a wry gin.

"You do look a bit out of place," she grinned back.

"Warriors ride or run or fight, they are not passengers. I will mount up when we leave the village."

"But you'll ride close to the carriage, won't you?"

"Of course. Don't worry, Lizbett, I will make sure no harm will come to you."

Settling back in her seat she sighed happily. It was strange being so far away from home, but it was thrilling and fun, and her thoughts began to move forward.

I'll be the wife of a warrior and a Commander. So much more exciting than some boring noble. I wonder what will happen when I take the throne? We must live in Verdana, but we could holiday in Zanderone. It's going to be interesting to see his house. I hope he has servants, I have to have servants.

"We're approaching the village," he remarked breaking into her thoughts.

"I'm so glad, I need to stretch, and I want to check on Scarlet."

The carriage began to slow, and she peered out at the modest homes as they came into view. They were similar to the houses in the villages in Verdana, but their gardens were full of blossoming flowers and small shrubs.

"Why are there so many more plants here than at home?" she asked wishing the blooms in the castle grounds were as abundant.

"It's the sun and the rain they get here. It's the same reason the barren land is so arid. It's very moderate in Verdana, but here it is very wet, giving life to the ground, and then for reasons we don't understand, the rain stops when it reaches the barren lands."

"They have no water?"

"They have times when they have more water than anywhere else, and then it's very dangerous, but the marauders have learned how to store it. The communities are quite green, but it only through careful planning."

The carriage rolled to a stop, and Larian stood up and opened the door, stepping out and stretching.

"Come along, Lizbett," he said extending his arm to take her hand.

As she lifted her dress to climb out they both saw the tell-tale stain on her petticoat, and she began to giggle.

"I don't think you should wash that off," he whispered. "Not ever."

"I think I agree," she whispered back.

He guided her forward as the warriors dismounted and immediately began unsaddling their horses. Seeing Scarlet on the opposite side of the carriage she rushed forward to pet her.

"Scarlet, are you all right?"

Scarlet looked at her with bright eyes, but didn't paw at the ground as she usually did when she wasn't moving.

"She's doing very well, Princess," Zoltaire said. "She's enjoying herself, but all the horses need water and some food, so we're taking them over to the stables there."

He pointed across at a stableyard beside the inn.

"We'll be back to eat and drink ourselves once we know the horses are taken care of."

Lizbett patted her neck, and Scarlet dropped her head and nudged her in response.

"She does look happy," she remarked, "and really calm. I've never seen her so calm. She must be tired."

"She is, a bit," Larian said as Zoltaire took the lead rope and led her away next to his own horse, "but that's good. Do you see how the men take care of their horses before themselves?"

"I did notice that," she replied.

"Their mounts carry them into battle, they transport them across great distances, they give them warmth at night, they are precious to us."

"Warmth at night? How?"

"They will lay with us, sleep with us, and even though they have a flight instinct, they will fight against wild animals to protect us."

"Wow, that's amazing."

"If you want to have that with Scarlet, I can teach you."

"Yes, please, definitely."

"When we reach my house it will be part of your training," he promised, then placing his hand at her back, he guided her inside the inn and settled at a table.

"Lizbett," he whispered, "I forgot to mention, you are not a Princess here, you are just a genteel lady."

"Why?"

"You have forgotten about the recent events already?" Think about it."

Sitting back in her chair she let out a small grunt.

"Oh, of course."

A large woman with a round face and very red cheeks bustled towards them.

"Welcome, my name is Alianda. I can offer you meat cooked in broth, fowl cooked in broth, or broth."

"Only those three things?" Lizbett asked staring at her in amazement.

"We have some breads and cheese," the rotund woman suggested.

"I am Commander Larian Lobergene and I am traveling with six men. They'll be coming in here soon, and need to have their bellies filled, so please bring them as much as they ask for. I'll have the meat in broth, and for my lady, Tebzilla, the fowl in broth."

"I believe these must be your men now, Commander," she remarked watching the six brawny men wander in and settle into a table. "From Zanderone I see."

"Yes, we are."

"You have many friends here, Sir. Your kingdom keeps the marauders away from our village, and we are very thankful."

"We do our best," he smiled.

The woman waddled away, and Lizbett reached across the table and grabbed his arm.

"Tebzilla? You keep the marauders at bay?"

"I can't call you Lizbett, and Tebzilla is almost Lizbett backwards."

"I suppose," she grimaced, "but what's this about the marauders?"

"We don't have to do it anymore, but a while back they were sneaking into this village at night, stealing from the kitchens and storehouses. They didn't hurt anyone, but my Prince heard about it and sent us to stop them. It was only for a short time."

"What did you do?" she asked eager to hear the story.

"We slightly injured a few to show them we could hurt them, but then we provided them with some grains and animals and taught them how grow their own vegetables and use their animals."

"If you did all that, why would they have stopped the carriage on the way to Verdana?"

"Because not all the marauders wanted our help. There is an aggressive offshoot, and the younger men are rebellious. They are a concern for this village, and other realms as well. They're not a threat yet, but they could be one day."

"But Zanderone and Verdana will stop them if they become difficult, right?"

"Probably, but relations between realms can change."

"I know what you mean. Verdana and Zanderone weren't always friends, that's what father says."

"But we are now, and that's why it's important to keep my Prince informed, because someone may be trying to stir up trouble between us, or hurt us both so one cannot come to the other's aid."

"One day it will be me who has to consider all these things," she remarked solemnly. "I'm so glad you'll be there to advise me."

"Our union will cement our kingdoms," he smiled, "and together we will be strong."

"Larian," she said tilting her head to one side.

"Yes, Tebzilla?"

"Don't call me that," she whispered brusquely.

"I certainly will if I wish," he replied raising one scolding eyebrow. "What is it you want to ask me?"

"When I am Queen, I will be the ruler. That means everyone must do as I tell them, right?"

"Yes, that's right," he grinned knowing exactly what she was about to say.

"So, if you and I are married, and I'm the Queen, then you'll have to obey me. If I order you to do something, you'll have to do it."

His grin grew wider and he leaned across table, locking her eyes.

"You want to order me about? You're welcome to try."

The flippity flip somersaulted in her stomach, and swallowing hard she dropped her eyes to the table.

Why does he make me feel this way? Now all I want to do is to lay in his lap and have him touch my nugget.

"When we reach my uncle's home I will take care of your hungry nugget."

"How did you know?" she asked snapping her head up, her eyes wide.

"I know many things, and you'd best remember that."

CHAPTER SIXTEEN

Though Alianda wanted no payment for the meal Larian insisted.

"My men consumed a great deal," he said pushing coins into the woman's hand. "Perhaps if I stop in again one day, you might provide me with some tea."

"Tea, Sir? I shall provide you with much more than that," she exclaimed, and with a warmth that filled his heart she hugged him as tightly as her body would allow. "We are so indebted to your Prince, please tell him so."

A short while later Lizbett was safely settled in her seat, Larian was astride Thunder, and the carriage and its retinue pulled away from the inn and headed down the road that would take them into the barren land.

It wasn't long before she noticed the landscape changing; the village had been thick with lush foliage but it was quickly disappearing, replaced by plants that looked grey and brown. Even the ground was different, no longer covered in grass but dark cracked dirt. The carriage ride which had been relatively smooth became jarring and uneven, and the tenderness that remained across her bottom was feeling every bump.

"No wonder they call this the barren land," she muttered to herself as she gazed out the window. "It's awful out here."

The landscape had become completely flat and the only hills she could see were far in the distance. The temperature had changed as well; it was now hot, and she reached across and opened the small basket of food and drink her servant had packed for her. The fowl in broth at the inn hadn't tasted very good and she hadn't eaten much, so she started munching on the delicious items the castle kitchen had prepared.

"This is much better," she smiled downing a particularly tasty morsel, and taking a long drink of tea from a container that kept things cool, she let out a satisfied sigh.

The suns were high in the sky and seemed to be baking the ground, and as the time melted away she became bored and restless. There was no scenery to look at, she was overly warm, and the ride was an endless series of bumps that were rattling her nerves.

"Please let us get through this part soon," she groaned. "I hate the barren land."

She was just about to close her eyes and try to nap when she heard shouting, and startled, she slid across her seat and stared out at the nothingness; off in the distance she could see a plume of dust. The carriage abruptly halted almost jolting her to the floor; she saw Larian jump from Thunder, and a moment later he climbed inside.

"The marauders are coming. They've laid some shrubs across the road to block our way."

"Can't your men just move them?"

"No, it's not wise to be off our horses, and the marauders are approaching fast, besides, the carriage is slow, they will quickly catch us."

"How did they know we were coming?"

"I don't know they did, they may have just wanted to stop whoever happened along the road, but regardless it's time for you to hide, and quickly," he declared.

Pulling the soft cushions off the bench opposite her he lifted the seat and gestured for her to climb inside.

"In there?" she exclaimed. "You expect me to get in there?"

"Right now," he barked.

Moving closer she stared into the small space, then standing up straight she shook her head.

"No, it's impossible," she frowned. "You said you could fight them off with no trouble, so I'd rather you do that."

"Lizbett, this is no time..."

"I'm serious. I'm not crawling into that tiny space," she said vehemently, pointing at it defiantly.

Larian's hand shot forward and grabbed the bodice of her dress; with one powerful jerk he ripped it from her chest leaving her bounteous breasts for the world to see.

"AARRGGHH! WHAT HAVE YOU DONE?" she screamed frantically trying to cover herself.

"Unless you want the marauders and my men to see your lovely breasts, I suggest you get into your hiding place right away."

"I can't believe you did that," she wailed as she frantically tried to crawl into the narrow space and hold her arms across her chest at the same time.

"Needs must, now hurry up, they're almost upon us."

As she climbed in and was attempting to lay back he glanced around the carriage and spied her shawl still sitting on the seat. Hastily grabbing it he dropped it on top of her.

"I'm not comfortable, it's so cramped," she protested as she pulled the shawl over her chest. "I'll suffocate."

"There are plenty of air vents along the back side. Now be very quiet and be very still," he growled, then closing the seat he slid a secret bolt into place and put back the cushions. If anyone did get into the carriage and thought to test the top of the seat it wouldn't budge.

Taking a quick look around he saw nothing to suggest a woman had been there, but closed the hamper and placed it on the floor, then standing in the open doorway he grasped the top of the carriage, swung up his legs, and landed on the roof.

Standing tall with his hands on his hips, the sun glinting off the steel that hung around various parts of his body and the long sheath that held his sword, the stance gave him two advantages; he would look bigger than life as the marauders approached, and he would be able to scan them as they came close, calculating their number and prowess.

His men formed a straight line in front of the carriage with Zoltaire in the center by the carriage door; their horses were still but snorting, knowing they may soon be asked to charge forward.

Larian quickly saw the marauders numbered a dozen, all dressed in the hooded cloaks they wore as protection from the sun. The leader was out front with two men flanking him just slightly back, while the remaining nine lagged behind in no particular formation. Scrutinizing their bodies he noted the only weapons they carried were various clubs hanging from ropes around their waists.

"Your business," Larian called, his voice booming from the top of the carriage.

"Give us your food and valuables, and whatever you carry in the carriage, and we will move the obstacles in your path and let you pass," the leader called back as he ventured forward.

"I have another offer," Larian declared. "Move the obstacles and we will let you live."

"You are outnumbered," the leader yelled. "We are double your men."

"I will instruct my warriors to remain with the carriage. I need some sport and I will kill each of you by myself."

As he'd spoken Larian's eyes had been surveying the unruly group of men determining which were the weakest. At the very back he'd caught a glimpse of reddish hair falling out from under a hood, and the tiniest glint of steel poking out below the cloak; without warning the precognitive thought flashed through his head.

An opportunity to help the King will present itself.

The answer came to him in a flash; the treacherous nobles who had escaped had approached the marauders and convinced them to stop the carriage.

They must have learned the Princess would be traveling, or did they just want our swords and horses?

"Let us see inside your carriage," the leader repeated.

"You alone, you approach. I am a Warrior Of The First Order and a Commander. I give you my word no harm will come to you."

It was universally understood that if a Warrior Of The First Order gave his word it could be trusted. The warriors were men of honor, and their word, especially the Warriors Of The First Order, was gold.

The leader didn't move, so without warning Larian made a spectacular leap from the top of the carriage over the heads of the horses and his men, landing safely on the ground in front of them. He was rewarded by an uneasy murmuring that rustled through the group of the unkempt men.

Larian had executed the stunt to shock them, show his athleticism, and intimidate the leader into doing his bidding; it worked; the leader moved his horse forward.

"Please, dismount. You may come and see inside the carriage. We are warriors, but we prefer to settle matters reasonably. I give you my word, no harm will come to you," then pausing he added, "my name is Larian Lobergene."

Larian had changed his voice from deep and commanding, to warm and cajoling.

"My name is Zanock," the marauder nervously replied. "I believe the word of a warrior, but..."

"Please," Larian said, and gestured for Zoltaire to move his horse so they could enter the carriage.

He knew the marauder was still skeptical so Larian turned his back on him as a sign of trust as he opened the carriage door.

"See, there's nothing in here," Larian said stepping aside, "come and see for yourself."

As Zanock first peered, then climbed inside, Larian pulled his sword and held it in the air to give to Zoltaire, but as he did he signaled Zoltaire to lean forward.

"Stay by the door and listen as we talk," he said softly as he handed him his weapon.

Zoltaire nodded, and as Larian climbed into the carriage Zoltaire dismounted and stood beside the door.

Zanock had sensed there was more to Larian's invitation than to simply verify that the carriage was empty, and though cautious the marauder was curious.

"Zanock, thank you. I suspect you guessed I need to speak with you privately."

"I did, but this is a strange turn," he replied.

"Some men came to you, noble, wealthy men, and offered you many things if you would join forces with them against the King of Verdana."

"How do you know this?" Zanock frowned.

"I am a Commander, it is my business to know," Larian replied. "There are things I should tell you about these men, but if you would rather not hear what I have to say you may leave."

"I wish to hear," Zanock said.

Larian sat back in his seat and paused, studying the man in front of him.

I was right. The nobles are with the marauders. If nothing else I can send word to the King but Zanock appears to be reasonable. Perhaps I can achieve more.

"The men who approached you are evil," Larian began. "They will use you to get what they want, and if they let you live, which is very doubtful, they will only do so to enslave you and your families. Please, tell me, what did they say was in the carriage that they wanted so badly?"

"A woman," Zanock replied, "a very important woman, but they didn't say who."

The did know we were coming through here with the Princess, but how?

"As you can see there is no woman," Larian continued.

Zanock looked around; there was no evidence that anyone had been traveling inside.

"This carriage came through before with food for the King, my gift to him."

"Yes, it was stopped by some foolish young men who do not understand the strength of the Zanderone warriors."

"You know my men could easily have killed them, but they didn't because they are men of honor. They kill only if defending themselves."

Zanock stared out the window as if pondering, then looked back at Larian.

"I know this," he said quietly.

"But the nobles you harbor, Zanock, they will do you and your families harm, great harm."

"Tell me more. Why did they leave the King?"

"They tried to poison a King they claimed to love, but their plot failed and they know if they're caught they will be executed. Everything they ask is for them, not for you."

Larian paused, then leaned forward.

"Zanock, listen very carefully. You know the warriors of Verdana and the warriors of Zanderone are powerful and have strong weapons. No matter your numbers you will suffer great losses and will be defeated. Do not let these four cowardly men push you to your deaths; do not leave your wives without husbands, and your children without fathers."

"I believe your words, Larian Lobergene, and I already knew these things when they approached me," Zanock admitted, "but with great worry I felt compelled to help them."

"Why? What did they offer you that could be so potent? Was it great riches?"

"We are a simple people, riches are of no use to us. Food, animals, this is what we seek, but that is not what drove me to comply."

Larian saw the defeat in the man's eyes, but he saw something else; it was a deep sadness.

"What is it?"

"My son, he is very sick. They offered medicine. They said if I captured the woman in the carriage they would pay me with medicine for my son."

Larian leaned back in his seat; now it made sense.

"Tell me about your son, how is he sick?"

"He has the hot beads of water on his forehead, and he coughs, he can hardly breathe. He has been this way for many passes of the moons."

"I believe I know this illness and I have something that might help him," Larian offered. "I cannot promise, but if anything can cure him it's this."

"Why would you help me? I am a marauder. I was going to-"

"You are also a man," Larian interrupted, "with a son who is sick. These evil men chose to push into something you didn't wish to do in exchange for the medicine. I will give you the medicine freely. It is with Zoltaire, the leader of my guards."

Larian traveled with remedies in case any of his men fell ill, and Zoltaire was charged with their safekeeping. Leaning out the carriage door Larian touched him on the shoulder.

"Give me the cure for the chest sickness."

Flipping open a bag hanging from his saddle, Zoltaire retrieved a small small vial containing a thick green syrup and gave it to Larian.

"Place a fingertip of this under the boy's tongue every quarter move of the East sun and the moons," Larian instructed handing over to Zanock. "Do this for five passes of the moons and he should be better, and take this too," he added grabbing the hamper. "There is not much in here, just some things given to us for the journey. It is good food, give it to your son to aid his healing."

Zanock stared at Larian, his eyes clouding over.

"I am humbled and shamed," he said somberly.

"I have no children," Larian replied, "but I know in my heart that when I do, I will go to any lengths to keep them well."

"What should I do with the nobles?"

"They are your guests, or prisoners as you wish. Do with them what you will, but the King would be relieved if they were no longer a threat."

"I shall return them to the King myself, but can you assure me of our safety when we deliver them?"

"I will send one of my men back to the castle to inform the King you will be arriving with the traitors, and not only will you be safe, you will return with a reward."

"This medicine…and the respect you have shown me…this is my reward," Zanock said soberly, then pausing he added, "there is something you should know. There is a traitor still in the castle. She came to our camp last night and told the nobles about the woman in the carriage."

"She?" Larian asked. "Who is this person? What is her name?"

"I'm sorry, I barely heard it, but I think it was, perhaps, Dinele."

"Delina?"

"Yes, Delina."

"Thank you, Zanock, now go in peace."

"The people from Zanderone and Verdana will never be disturbed by my men again," Zanock promised, "unless it is by the youth. Sometimes the young ones are hard to control."

"I know this well," Larian smiled.

Climbing from the carriage Zanock hurried to his horse and cantered back to his group, and as Larian was ensuring Thunder was properly tethered to the carriage he saw two of the marauders gallop down to the brush that had blocked the road and begin to clear it.

"You should be leading a realm," Zoltaire remarked as Larian returned. "You should be a King."

"Opportunity is everywhere," Larian replied. "You just have to keep your eyes and ears open. Now you must make haste back to the King and tell him everything you heard. Also tell him I suggest food and medicines as a reward, and some animals if he deems it."

"Yes, Commander."

"Then meet us back at my uncle's home."

"Yes, Commander."

"Is the mare safe to travel alongside Thunder?"

"Yes, she has completely settled."

"Good. Tether her and have the driver move us out at a safe but good speed as soon as the brush is fully cleared. Travel safe, Zoltaire."

Stepping inside the carriage he peered out the window and saw several of the marauders circle the noble; the hooded cloak was pulled off and his sword, now revealed, removed from its sheath.

With the brush out of the way the carriage began to roll forward, and waiting until the marauders were out of sight, their dust barely visible, Larian pulled the shades to cover the windows, then moved the cushions from the seat and lifted the lid; Lizbett stared up at him.

"I heard everything," she murmured slowly sitting up. "You were amazing."

"Thank you, and now, Lizbett, your bottom, your *bare* bottom, is going to feel just hot how my hand can be."

CHAPTER SEVENTEEN

Wrapping the shawl around her, Lizbett stared pleadingly at Larian as he helped her from the tight cubicle.

"Please, not bare, please," she begged.

"Yes, you deserve it, you put us in danger. I'm surprised at you," he scolded.

"But I-"

"There is no excuse, none," he declared pulling her out of the way as he closed the seat and put back the cushions.

"Please may I at least put on a fresh dress?"

"No, your breasts will stay bared, they will will also suffer punishment," he said sternly, and grabbing her wrist he moved her to stand at his side as he sat down.

"What? Noooo, not my breasts."

"The more you protest and argue the greater will be your discipline," he warned. "You know you were extremely bad. Not only did you refuse to do as I said at a crucial time, you wanted to put my men into battle just so you wouldn't be uncomfortable for a short while."

"I...uh..."

"Exactly, there is nothing you can possibly say in your defense. You must be punished and punished properly. Remove your shawl."

"Sir," she whimpered.

She was embarrassed; he had fondled her breasts but they had never been exposed to his eye.

"Do not make me wait!" he barked.

Sighing deeply, she dropped the shawl from her shoulders and let it fall to the floor.

"That's better," he growled, then lifting his hand he pinched her nipples…hard.

"OW!"

"When we are at my home I have special tools to deal with naughty nipples," he declared.

"Why do you call them naughty?" she bleated.

"Because you are naughty, therefore every part of your body is open for punishment. Your nipples, your breasts, your nugget-"

"No, not that," she protested, her eyes wide.

"Especially that," he said sternly. "Enough, lift your dress and petticoats and lay over my lap. Your bottom is about to feel my displeasure."

Uttering strange whimpering sounds she gathered the folds of her dress and flouncy farthingales and dropped her body over his thighs, but unhappy with her position he placed his wide hands around her waist and lifted her off his lap.

"Sir!"

"Hush, you are to be further over, no resting your head on the cushions, reach your hands to the floor."

"Oh, Sir, this is so uncomfortable."

"As it should be," he declared positioning her as he wished. "There, now grip my ankle for support, and do not move your hands from there until I tell you. Do you understand?"

"Yes, Sir."

Studying the thin silky undergarment covering her backside, he paused, considering how divine it would be to finally rest his eyes on her full, round cheeks. He had thought the unveiling would be at his home in front of a flaming fireplace, with wine and food nearby, and kisses and fond touches, but her behavior warranted his spanking hand on her skin, and so it would be.

Finding the cord that held them in place he realized it was knotted in the front, and not wishing to deal with it he pulled his short knife from its holder.

"Hold still," he warned.

Slipping the blade under the garment and turning it up against the thin rope he jerked it towards him, slicing easily through the cord. Depositing the knife back into the holder, he grasped the thin fabric, and with a sharp tug on either side he ripped it apart; her bottom, exposed for the first time, gazed up at him.

"Ooh, Sir," she mewled.

Pushing the frayed material to either side he relished the sight, then pondered the fading horizontal lines left by the crop the afternoon before.

"I am going to spank you hard, Lizbett, very hard. You may call out but it will not stop me. I intend for you to learn this lesson. You will never question my orders when we are in danger, never!"

"I won't, I've learned," she cried, "I swear."

His hand abruptly slapped leaving an instant red imprint, then quickly slapped again causing her to kick out. Lifting his heavy leg he placed it over the backs of her knees, then placing his palm firmly around her waist he gripped tightly.

"Now you will understand what it means to be punished by a warrior. Truly punished. After this you will never again risk life or limb, never again, and I repeat myself because it's necessary you understand. Never again!"

"No, Sir, never," she repeated, "I already-"

Before she could finish his hand began to rain its swats slowly and forcefully upon her upturned, naked cheeks. His rhythm was deliberate, his stinging palm landing blow after blow, covering every part of her backside. She wailed and wriggled but her gyrations were no match for his hold, and when his spanking traveled to the sweet crease where her thighs touched her bottom, her wailing turned to howls for mercy.

Pausing, he stared at her scorched, splotchy skin, and dropping his hand he searched out her breasts to tweak her nipples.

"Ooww, Sir, please, please, I beg you."

He pinched again, harder.

"OW, OW!"

"I'm not finished with your very bad bottom," he growled, "but I will be shortly, then your bad breasts will be next."

What followed was a volley of fast, hard spanks, starting at the back of her thighs, moving on to her cheeks, then back down, sending her gasping and furiously squirming. When he stopped, he fiercely gripped each cheek.

"Burning?"

"Oh, yes, Sir," she whimpered. "Like embers from a fire."

"Sit up and straddle my lap."

Panting and uttering sounds of pain, she struggled to stand up, then sat across his wide thighs, and as his hands clutched her waist to bring her forward, she dropped her head into his shoulder.

"You have punished me so hard, Sir," she groaned.

"And you tested me so hard," he replied. "It is one thing to be willful and petulant in normal life, but to refuse an order given in a moment of such jeopardy and suggest my men risk injury, perhaps even death, is not just the height of self-centered selfishness, it is reckless, irresponsible and outrageous," he scolded.

"You're right, you're so right, I am very ashamed."

Clutching a fistful of her hair he yanked her head from his shoulder and sent his eyes to hers, but they remained downcast.

"Look at me."

Slowly she raised her gaze, and when their eyes touched she felt a swell of emotion.

"Everything you accused me of is true," she bleated. "It's like I said before, I'm not good enough for you."

"Stop that," he said tenderly. "You are just extremely spoiled. You need to be trained and you will be, and you must understand I do not wish to punish you so severely, but your crime was grievous and I must discipline you as necessary."

"Yes, Sir, I know, and again I can only say I don't know why I do these things."

"I am a Commander. My men were just outside the carriage. That a slip of a girl would dare question me, even a Princess, it cannot be allowed and must be swiftly dealt with."

"I don't know what to say," she whimpered.

"Your stinging backside will not be your only punishment. When we reach my uncle's home there will be further discipline."

"More spanking?" she whispered a deep crease crossing her brow.

"No, and it's not something you've yet been subjected to, but enough of that. Put your hands behind your back and thrust out your breasts. I see you are over your embarrassment about me viewing them."

"My shame and the pain of my bottom are my only thoughts," she moaned as she clasped her fingers behind her back.

Curling her hair around his fingers he pulled slowly, forcing her head back, then lowering his lips to one of her puckered nipples he began to suck.

Initially she thought it a heavenly respite. His warm mouth was intoxicating, and as he drew the nipple further in and against his tongue, she thought she would swoon with pleasure…but there was no pause; the pleasant sensation began to dissolve into an odd pain.

"Sir, please," she begged.

He yanked on her hair and sucked even harder, and just when she thought she could bear it no more he stopped.

"As red as your bottom," he remarked staring at the crimson flush around her nipple, "and I am impressed that you didn't unlock your fingers. You have just won a small amount of forgiveness."

"Sir," she mewled, "this is very painful."

"Now to the twin," he declared ignoring her complaint.

Lowering his lips to the opposite breast he started the soft, gentle attention, then slowly increased the vacuum until she was again pleading for him to stop. He measured the time between her plea and when he chose to pull back, pushing her to the limit of her endurance, then stopped and released her hair.

"On to your knees in front of me," he said sternly.

She was as desperate to hold her searing seat cheeks as she was to rub her painful breasts, and choosing the latter she slipped off his thighs and knelt before him.

"Hands at your sides," he said firmly. "Now tell me, what you have to say for yourself?"

"Sir, I am so sorry for questioning you at such a critical time. I am a foolish, selfish girl and should never have suggested your warriors fight so I wouldn't have to hide. It was wrong of me, very wrong. All I can do is pray that you'll forgive me."

"Anything else?"

"Yes, Sir, thank you for punishing me. I needed it, and I wanted it."

"Good," he sighed. "You may crawl into my lap and be comforted, but the third part of your punishment awaits."

Crawling back into his lap she curled into a ball as he held her. With gentle caresses he helped alleviate the pain in her breasts, then kissing her softly he murmured in her ear.

"I love you, Lizbett, I only punish you because I love you."

"I know, Sir," she sighed.

"Can you feel the carriage ride is smoother?"

"I didn't notice, Sir, but yes, I feel it is."

"We are out of the barren land. It won't be long before we reach my uncle's house. Is your dress in the bag in the compartment at the back of the carriage?"

"Yes, Sir."

"I believe we are both thirsty. I shall have us stop for a moment and fetch it for you, along with some water. Cover yourself with your shawl."

Moving from his lap she retrieved the wide scarf from the floor and wrapped it around her shoulders, and once she was settled he lifted the shades from the windows. The landscape was once again lush and full; the barren land was behind them.

CHAPTER EIGHTEEN

A s the carriage rolled down a lane between tall trees, in spite of her sore bottom and aching breasts, Lizbett was full of wonder. Beauty surrounded her, and the animals she could see prancing around the fields beyond the trees made her want to jump from the carriage so she could run and join them. As they approached the stable yard she could hear Scarlet whinnying, and she broke into a smile.

"Scarlet wants to make new friends."

"And she shall, as will you," Larian said warmly.

The carriage rolled to a stop and Lizbett waited for Larian to climb out, then taking his hand she stepped daintily on to the soft dirt; she was arriving as Princess Lizbett of Verdana, and she wanted to impress his uncle.

Looking around she saw a splendid barn, horses fenced in oversized pens giving them plenty of room to wander and graze, and several young men were bustling around doing their chores. Scarlet was still whinnying, and Lizbett moved quickly to the back of the carriage to check on her. When the mare spied her she let out a snort and began pawing at the ground.

"She is still impatient, even after that long journey," Larian remarked. "I will take her to a field next to other horses. She can play at the fence but it's better she's by herself. She could start a fight with her excited mood."

"Scarlet just likes to let me know how she feels," Lizbett protested.

"Scarlet is as spoiled as her owner," Larian whispered, and untying the lead rope he briskly walked the horse across the yard to a small empty field. Lizbett hurried to keep up, but her soft shoes were made only to look pretty and grace a planked dance floor, not to walk in dirt.

"Your uncle won't mind?" she asked reaching the gate just as Larian let the mare loose.

"This field is for guest horses, he won't mind a bit."

"Of course I won't mind."

The voice was old and husky, and turning around Lizbett saw an elderly man striding towards them. Though his age showed in his face, his body was straight and tall, his shoulders square, and she could see how he was once a warrior, just like her beloved Larian.

"How is my favorite nephew?" he beamed. "My Warrior Of The First Order, my Commander. I'm so proud of you. Any trouble on the way?"

"I have much news, Uncle," Larian said gravely, "news that must be shared over food and wine, but first, please meet Princess Lizbett of Verdana, the woman I am to marry."

"Ahhh, so happy is this news. It is lovely to meet you, Princess. I am acquainted with your father. We once shared some hazardous times. He is an exceptional man, and an exceptional leader. I believe I did meet you once, when you were just a little girl."

"It is lovely to meet you too, Uncle...?"

"Just Uncle," he smiled, "everyone calls me Uncle. I don't even remember what my name is anymore," he chuckled. "Come into the house, I am eager to hear about this news, Larian. Your men will be fed and housed in the warrior's quarters, but of course you know that," then slapping him on the back he added, "Larian, my boy, I am just so pleased you're here."

"I am too, Uncle, it has been too long and we have much to discuss," Larian replied. "Perhaps Lizbett should go straight to her chamber so she can freshen up and get some rest."

"Ah, yes, women should do this after a long journey," he nodded. "They need to lay down, they need to gather themselves."

Lizbett was about to protest, to say she was fine, she didn't need to go anywhere and she wanted to stay with them, but before she could utter a word Larian shot her a look and the message in his aqua eyes was clear;

I want to be alone with my uncle for a while, go to your room and stay there until I call for you.

Swallowing back her argument, she graciously said,

"Thank you, Uncle, for understanding the needs of a woman."

Looking at Larian she was rewarded with a smile that made her heart swell; she had pleased him, and after everything that had happened in the carriage she wanted to please him more than anything.

They had reached the house, a sprawling one-story building that had many windows and a large covered patio. As they walked inside Lizbett found herself in a reception area, and was astonished at the many artifacts surrounding her, but before she had time to ask about them a small woman hurried forward and curtsied.

"This is Adamine," Uncle said. "She will take care of you during your night here. Adamine, this is Princess Lizbett from Verdana, please show her to the guest room overlooking the back fields."

"Larian, will someone bring up my bag?" Lizbett asked softly.

"Of course, it will be delivered to your room shortly," he promised.

Adamine curtsied again, then without a word began to walk towards one of three hallways that led in different directions; realizing she was expected to follow Lizbett hurried after her.

"Lizbett is charming," his Uncle remarked quietly.

"Thank you, Uncle. May I ask, is there a tray of food in her room? She'll be starving."

"Oh, yes, an excellent meal is waiting," his Uncle assured him, "and no doubt she'll want to rest after eating."

"She will that," Larian sighed, "and thank goodness, I need a break. She's such a handful, literally. Sometimes she is as smart as her father, but other times…"

"But you have been taught how to handle women, especially those who have been raised as she has. Just keep her on a regular schedule of discipline and she'll be fine."

"Is her willful character so obvious?" Larian asked, surprised his Uncle had seen it in spite of Lizbett's good behavior when they'd arrived.

"No, but I saw her as a child. She was a terror, absolutely out of control, and from what I've heard nothing has changed."

"You're right, Uncle, nothing has changed. I have had to spank several times already."

"Like I said, make it regular, on a schedule.. Start every day with her over your lap, or at night before sleep. As her disposition improves you can make it once a week, but it has to be regular."

"Thank you, Uncle, I'll take your advice. I hadn't thought of that but yes, I think that would be a very good idea."

"Now, to the dining hall. I want to hear the news."

As the two men made their way down a long corridor, Lizbett was standing in her bed-chamber staring at the reflection of her very red backside.

Her bag had arrived moments after Adamine had shown her into the room. Though the small woman wanted to stay and help her change, or brush her long hair, Lizbett had dismissed her saying she needed to rest, but what she really wanted to do was look at her sore backside.

The reflecting glass showed her just how determined her warrior had been to exact his discipline. Crimson and dark purple blotches stained her cheeks, and when she turned around and lowered the front of her dress, she sighed when she stared at the redness surrounding her rosebud nipples.

"What will the third part of his discipline be?" she mumbled. "He'd said he was going to punish my nugget. What could he possibly mean?"

Moving into the ante-chamber she brushed her hair and washed up, then returning to the room she noticed a tray of food on a table in a far corner. She was famished, and though she was unsure if she would be dining with the men some time later, she sat down and began to eat.

It was a delicious feast, complete with wine, and when she was finished she wandered to the bed and laid down. It was supremely comfortable, the mattress soft and engulfing, and as a wave of fatigue washed over her she yawned several times then immediately fell asleep.

Sharing a meal with his uncle in the dining hall, Larian knew she'd be exhausted. Between the long journey, the lack of good food, the experience with the marauders, and his strong discipline, he'd had no doubt she'd fall asleep as soon as she stretched out to rest.

He and his uncle remained in the dining hall, talking until the two moons hung low in the dark sky, discussing family news as well as the events in Verdana.

"I am an old man, and even with Zinyana I now need sleep every night," his uncle sighed.

"Is it time for you to take to your bed?" Larian asked.

"I must, but before I retire, tell me, when and where do you plan to marry?"

"I will marry the Princess when I feel she is ready to be my wife, when her training is sufficient and she is deserving."

"Ha!"

Larian stared back at him, shocked at the scoffing retort.

"Uncle? I don't understand?"

"If that is your plan you will be waiting for many passages of the moon, and that will be too long…for both of you. A woman such as the Princess…her training will never stop. Her core is willful and rebellious. You need to marry her quickly, take her, own her, possess her, then you will be in a much more powerful position, then your training will have more substance."

Larian stared into his uncle's wise turquoise eyes and realized he was right; his own lack of insight was embarrassing, almost humiliating.

"Uncle, I feel so…"

"Uneducated? Inadequate? Immature?"

"All of those things. I feel as if you're my teacher, as if I'm back in training."

"You are. What you just told me obligates me to speak to you as a teacher. You have become a Commander, and your skills are exceptional, but you are still young. As a warrior you have had many women, you have had education in the ways of loving domination, the kind of domination that brings a happy marriage, but you have no practical experience with a woman for whom you care deeply. It was impossible. Your heart has belonged to Lizbett since you met her as a child."

"I wasn't a child," Larian declared.

"In the ways of men and women you were both children," his uncle frowned, "but that is not what we are discussing. Listen to me, pay attention."

"Yes, Uncle, I'm listening, and I apologize for my momentary lapse," Larian said quietly, then dropped his eyes as a mark of respect.

"You have already taught Lizbett about discipline, and you have the training and instincts to apply it properly, but you are just beginning to learn about such a woman. She is not just petulant, she is wily, and she will soon learn your ways…if she hasn't already. Believe me, Larian, there will come a day she will use that against you."

"But she loves me," Larian argued. "Why would she use anything against me?"

"It is her love that will cause her to. She wants to know you are smarter, wiser, and will catch her out. This is the danger.

Listen again. She is not just petulant, she is wily, and will soon learn your ways…if she hasn't already."

"So I must be on guard."

"Yes, you must be on guard."

"When you say, against me…"

"I mean, she will use her knowledge to get what she wants, but all the while you will be thinking you are in control."

"Oh, almost like strategy in battle. Maneuvering your opponent."

"Yes, Larian, just like that," his uncle nodded. "When you start to question yourself, that will be your warning. Then you must step away, take some time…one passage of the moons, or several…as long as it takes for you to look back and see the devious manipulation. Then you can return and show her she has not bettered you."

"Uncle, I hear the wisdom of your words."

"The punishments are necessary, and they will control her, but only to a point. True control comes from within her, from her love and wishing to please you, but that will only come from her respect for you."

"Yes, Uncle, I understand, I understand completely."

"This is why you must marry her soon. You do not doubt your devotion to each other, so why wait? You have chosen her. I repeat, you must take her, you must possess her with your body, then you will have the power to train her, properly train her."

"Ah, yes, I see," Larian nodded.

"I assume you must marry in Verdana."

"If things were settled, then yes, but a wedding, the celebrations, I'm not sure the King will feel it would be safe there, at least, not yet."

"Then, in Zanderone?"

"Perhaps, or perhaps at my new residence. Security would be much easier there, no crowds, just invited guests."

"This is better, to be married in the home where you can start your days together, away from the courts of your Prince and her father. This is the best path, Larian, if you can get blessings from both."

"Uncle, I am indebted to you, thank you."

"I care for you deeply, and since your father died you have been a son to me. He must be so proud as he looks down from the heavens."

"I strive to make him so every day," Larian said softly.

"He was the greatest warrior Zanderone has ever seen. You have inherited his gifts, and now you are marrying a Princess. One day you will rule Verdana at her side, but..."

"But first I must be sure I rule her," Larian finished.

"Exactly," the old man said, smiling and nodding his head, "and now I must retire."

They stood up from the table and Larian walked him to the hallway and hugged him warmly. As he watched the elderly warrior stride away, so tall and proud, he felt his heart swell.

"Thank goodness for you, Uncle," he murmured. "I almost made a grave error, thank goodness for you."

CHAPTER NINETEEN

The West sun had barely set when Lizbett had fallen asleep, and when the creak of her opening door stirred her to life she saw the darkness of night.

I have slept for so long, I must have been exhausted.

Rolling over she stared across the room, then smiled as she saw the outline of her warrior.

"My love," he whispered moving across and sitting on the edge of the bed.

"I didn't mean to sleep so long," she yawned, "but I was so tired."

"And still?" he asked.

"A little. How is your uncle?"

"He is the wisest man I know," Larian replied, "and I love him deeply."

"Are you here to say goodnight?"

"I am here to check on you, to stroke your body for a short time, to kiss you, to tell you how I love you, and…"

"And?"

"You know the and," Larian said softly.

"The third part of my punishment," she sighed. "I thought you had forgotten."

"I will never forget such a thing," he said solemnly, "but you are still dressed and you must be without clothing."

"You mean, completely?"

"I have seen your bottom and I have seen your breasts, why are you shocked?"

"Because you haven't seen the most private parts of me," she whispered.

"Of course I have, I saw all as you wriggled when I spanked you."

"You did?"

"I did, now get up and take everything off."

"Will you take your clothes off too?"

"Lizbett…"

"Sorry, sorry," she said quickly, and standing from the bed she began to peel off her dress.

The only light was from the twin moons, and their glow bathed the room in their pink-tinged silver radiance causing her skin to glisten, and as he stood, watching her undress, his member surged to life.

I want to take you right here, I want to thrust deep into your hot, wet, channel, I want to take you and make you mine, completely mine. Uncle was right. My plan to wait was foolish. I will keep you chaste until our wedding night, but that will be soon, very soon.

Her last petticoat fell from her shoulders, and untying the cord around her waist that held up her thin, silky underwear, she let it drop away then turned to face him.

"You are magnificent," he breathed.

Unbuckling his waist belt that held his small weapons and a bag he laid it on a table, then moving across the room he lifted her into his arms and laid her on the bed.

"Spread your legs, I am going to examine you."

"Oh, Sir," she purred, "those words send a shiver right through me."

Sitting alongside her hips he moved his fingers to open her slit, exposing her tiny nugget and the soft inner flesh. She gasped as he touched where his cock would one day travel, and when his thumb circled her nub she moaned and twisted, overcome with the ripples of sensation tingling through her sex.

"Why does that make me feel so much?" she bleated.

"Because it is the core of your need," he purred, "now shush, you must stop speaking and just feel."

"Is this the discipline?"

His hand landed with a sharp slap on her thigh, causing her to squeal in pain and surprise.

"What did I tell you? Be quiet...be quiet and feel."

"Ow, ow," she whispered, "ooowwww."

Larian smoothed his palm across the pink sore spot where his stinging swat had landed.

She has to learn, but it seems every time I give her an order she does the opposite and I have to slap her, or punish her somehow.

The thought gave him pause, and he made a mental note to think upon it later. Returning to his task he held open her delicate folds of flesh with one hand, while he used the fingers of the other to tease and toy.

In his training he had been taught many techniques to bring a woman to the brink of her moment, and playing with Lizbett, making her gasp and moan then bleat with disappointment, was making his cock leak in his trousers; it was supremely difficult to ignore, but he was a warrior, and he had learned to control the needs of his body, even such needs as his craving cock.

Stretching out alongside her he gently licked at a nipple as his finger swirled her nub, then he moved his mouth to her ear.

"Tell me, how does your nugget feel?"

"Please keep rubbing like that," she begged. "It needs it, I need it, I need to feel that amazing explosion and it's so close. The tingles have already begun."

"Ah, have they?" he whispered stilling his hand.

"Oh, Sir, why did you stop?"

"This is the third part of your discipline. I will leave you now, hungry like this."

"But it needs-"

"It needs to be taught who is in charge, who controls, and that is me, Lizbett, and to make sure you don't touch it after I leave I am going to tie you."

Rolling off the bed he moved quickly to the small bag attached to his waist belt and retrieved the soft cord he'd brought for the purpose, but as he turned to walk back he caught a glimpse of her hand quickly retreating from between her legs.

The earlier inkling suddenly flashed through his mind; *it seems every time I give her an order she does the opposite and I have to slap her, or punish her somehow.*

His instinct told him to ignore what he'd seen, and keeping his eyes low he pretended to study the rope as he sat on the edge of the bed, then leaned his head down and kissed her.

"Time for the rope," he murmured.

"Must you tie me?" she whimpered.

He did not answer, and sitting back he took her wrists and expertly laced the cord around them, tying off the two ends at the back of her waist; the bondage was loose enough that it wasn't uncomfortable, but would prevent her from touching herself.

"I believe that answers your question," he said firmly.

"What will Adamine think when she comes in to wake me?" she bleated.

"I require little sleep," he reminded her. "I will wander the grounds all night, travel all day tomorrow, and I will feel no fatigue."

"That is so amazing," she remarked.

"it is the simply the way of the Zanderone warrior," he replied. "Fear not, Lizbett, it will be me who will wake you, and I will hold you warmly against me as the East sun rises."

"You're leaving now?"

"I am, but I believe there are still some words you must say."

"Thank you, Larian, for your discipline. I deserve it, I need it, and I want it."

"Good girl," he crooned.

Leaning forward he scooped her into his chest and held her, rocking her gently, then laying her back down he pulled up the coverlets.

"One last thing," he murmured.

"Yes, Sir?"

"As you sleep think upon this question, and give me the answer when it comes to you, but only when you are sure of it. It doesn't have to be in the morning, it can be any time, but you must be sure of it."

"What question?"

"More than anything else, what makes you happy?"

He rose to his feet and stared down at her; the question he had put to her, and the answer he was seeking had come to him directly after talking with his uncle.

"Goodnight, Larian," she sighed.

"Goodnight, Lizbett," he replied tenderly, then picking up his waist belt he walked slowly from the room.

As he moved down the hallway to his chamber he sensed he was on the brink of an important discovery. Like a shadowy thought he couldn't quite grasp it, but he had learned to allow such things to float forward of their own accord; if he chased them they became evasive.

I must sleep a short while and perhaps the message will come. It is so close, I can feel it.

As Larian was thinking about the elusive epiphany, Lizbett was rubbing her thighs together, but she was also pondering his question;

More than anything else, what makes you happy?

But there are so many things. Riding Scarlet, eating tasty food, I'm happy after wine, getting presents, kissing you makes me really happy. You make me really happy. What is it you want me to say? This is a very difficult question.

Her thighs stopped their anxious rubbing, and as the moons continued their passage taking their pink-silver light from her chamber, she closed her eyes and drifted to sleep, a final thought crossing her mind.

Something important happened tonight, I'm just not sure what it is...

CHAPTER TWENTY

Larian had reached the doorway of his chamber, and though he needed to stroke himself and release the urgency in his trousers he felt a greater need to move out into the night. Making his way through the house he quietly unlocked the front door, slipped outside and stood in the quiet courtyard inhaling the cool night air. His senses were on alert, not because he felt lurking danger, but because, like Zinyana and so many other parts of his nature, it was an inherent trait.

He could cross a forest floor thick with dried leaves and sticks and not make a sound; he could hear a footfall when others could not; his eyes would adjust to changing light in an instant, he could lift boulders, climb the tallest tree, and bring a woman supreme pleasure. He could do all these things, and yet his uncle had needed to speak to him as a young, naive man.

It had humbled him, and standing under the two moons, gazing into the infinite ebony night, he realized he had needed to be humbled as much as Lizbett had needed his spanking hand. His meteoric rise had tilted his ego, an ego he had learned early in his training could be his undoing if not kept in check; were it not for his uncle he could have fallen victim to its clutches.

He needed to be with the horses. There was little that fed his soul like a still stable, whether it be day or night. As he ambled in, the smell of the hay and the soft, powerful, noble energy of the animals washed over him, calming his center and soothing his mind.

Settling on a bale of hay he thought back to the days when he would hold the youthful Lizbett in his arms amongst the billows of loose straw in the King's stables. Even then he had the ability to whisper and touch, to comprehend her moans and gasps.

You have done her no favors, Handerah, allowing her to grow into womanhood with no discipline, but somehow you have kept her innocent, sheltered from the ways of men. How did you manage that? She has a passionate soul, she aches for all a man can give her, and yet she knows so little, has experienced so little.

The image of her naked beauty bathed in the soft moon-glow sent a fresh wave of need through his loins, and unfastening the flap in the front of his trousers he withdrew his cock and began to rub.

Closing his eyes he saw her sweet rosebuds atop her large, perfect mounds; how delicious it had been to suck them until she was gasping. While the intense sensation might have been momentarily punishing, it would have fueled her sexual awakening and sent nurturing wet heat to the garden between her legs.

His moment was brewing and he rubbed vigorously, flashing back to the moment he had swished the crop upon her bottom after he'd found her fighting with Tholl. He had to smile as he recalled the surprise on her face when he'd arrived on the scene, and how quickly she had hurried away, knowing she would soon meet his chastisement.

Feeling the urgency in his cock and wanting to reach the end he indulged again in the fantasy of plunging into her succulent depths for the first time. He saw himself holding her hips and thrusting forward as she gasped and called his name, and suddenly his manhood jerked, shooting forth his cream. He groaned, fervently rubbing until the spasms began to abate, then dropping his hand away he laid back into the hay to catch his breath.

Nestled in the cloaking gentleness of the barn his heart's pounding began to settle, but the incident with Tholl floated back into his mind and he was struck by a thought.

Lizbett is not a stupid girl. She would have known Tholl would send for me.

Standing slowly he ambled to a water bucket and washed himself, thinking back over the journey in the carriage and her absurd request that the warriors fight so she wouldn't have to hide. With the urgency of the moment he done the only thing he could think of to get her into her hiding place, and not considered anything past the point of her atrocious behavior and the discipline he'd have to exact.

"...she will use her knowledge to get what she wants, but all the while you will be thinking you are in control."

Like a sharp bolt of lightening the epiphany struck.

"Lizbett! This is exactly what you have been doing!" he exclaimed to the empty barn. "You ache for discipline so much you have maneuvered events to have me deliver it. Our reunion at the bridge, our time in the meadow...that was a moment you had been seeking your entire life and once you tasted my spanking hand you wanted more...you needed more...you knew I would punish any misbehavior."

His discipline had become her reward.

The sound of a soft nicker called to him, interrupting his outburst, and turning around Larian was surprised to see Thunder's large black head peering over his door, his huge brown eyes staring straight at him.

The stalls in the stable opened into the barn, but also to large pens at the back so the horses could wander in and out as they pleased. Rarely did he see a horse in its shelter, the natural state of the outdoors was always preferable.

"Thunder," he smiled, and finding the bucket of carrots he grabbed a handful and carried them across to his noble steed. "My friend, you heard me."

The horse took the gift, munched loudly, then leaned the weight of his heavy head against Larian's chest.

"You calm me, you chase away the worry. Now I know why my instinct told me to ignore her hand between her legs earlier. She wanted more attention, more spanking or discipline of some kind. She is starving for it. Thunder, my uncle was right, she is wily, and she used what she learned to control me. There is much I must ponder through the remainder of this night."

Thunder softly nuzzled him, as if understanding everything Larian had just said.

"I am glad of one thing. I did not need to be away from her for a full passage of the moon to see this. I have no wish to be away from her for any length of time, but I understand what my uncle meant. I would not have seen clearly had I been laying beside her. I would have been captivated by her body, I would have been thinking only of the joy of being with her."

Thunder pricked his ears, and a moment later Larian heard it too; the distant sound of approaching hooves.

"Who would be coming here so late?" he frowned, and giving Thunder another stroke on his neck he moved out into courtyard.

His keen hearing told him he wouldn't have long to wait; whoever was riding was galloping at top speed. Looking across to the fields he saw the horses moving around, anticipating the arrival, and he could see Scarlet bucking in her paddock.

While he didn't anticipate an adversary he didn't feel comfortable waiting alone with no sword at his side, so he hurried over to the warrior's house. Opening the door carefully, not wishing to disturb anyone who might be in Zinyana, he spied two of his men quietly chatting and sharing some wine in a corner. They looked up as he entered, and he signaled for them to join him and bring their swords; moments later the three were headed back to the courtyard.

"I hope it's not bad news," one of them remarked.

"Whoever it is, he is very close," the other added.

Practiced in the art of defense they immediately separated so each would have a third of the courtyard, and while Larian remained visible his two men stayed hidden. He heard the horse break from its gallop into a trot, and a short time later it entered the courtyard; Larian immediately broke into a broad smile.

"Zoltaire!"

"Commander!" the warrior hailed in reply as he leapt from his horse.

"I'm glad to see you," Larian declared. "You must have traveled with great haste to be back so soon."

"I was anxious to bring you the news," Zoltaire declared.

The warriors who had been hiding appeared from their covert positions and hurried across to welcome him. Larian was eager to hear the report, but knowing the two men and Zoltaire needed a moment for a reunion, he took the horse into the stables and began to take off his saddle. The camaraderie between the three was essential; in battle they were brothers, each fighting for the other, and the small moments mattered. He had just put the horse into an empty stall and filled its water bucket when Zoltair entered the barn.

"I have much to tell you," he said quickly.

"Let us go into the kitchen and sit at a table. You must need food and wine."

"It would be good," he nodded, and together they crossed the courtyard and headed into the house.

CHAPTER TWENTY-ONE

The kitchen was well stocked, and as Zoltaire removed his sword, waist belt and heavy jacket, Larian plated cheese, bread, some fruit and nuts, and some slices of meat left over from the dinner he'd shared with his uncle. There were several bottles of wine on the counter, and selecting the one that contained the most he set it on the table along with two goblets.

"This cheese is excellent," Zoltaire declared. "I am never hungry until I begin to eat."

"The warrior's curse and blessing," Larian remarked. "Now, please, tell me what news you have brought."

"The King was greatly heartened by the news that the marauders were bringing the escaped nobles to the castle. He looked weary, Larian, and I feel the absence of the Princess has been difficult, but shortly after I arrived his wife rolled up in her carriage, and that brightened him."

"I can imagine the King would be missing Lizbett very much," Larian said thoughtfully.

"The King told me that the plot to kill him had been long in the planning, but they could only execute their evil deed while the Queen was away."

"Why?"

"Because she is famous for her sense of smell. Their only chance was the poison, and she would surely have detected it.

Apparently few know that the Princess inherited her mother's gift."

"So my being there…"

"…while the Queen was out of town gave them their chance. They'd been waiting for a banquet, and your arrival happened to coincide with her absence."

"What happened with Delina?" Larian asked, recalling the handsome woman who had appeared so warm and capable when he'd arrived.

"Delina had no stomach for interrogation, and just before I left I heard that in exchange for a quick death she has promised to tell all she knows, so I suspect there is even more news by now."

"And did the marauders arrive while you were there?"

"They did, Larian. I had met with the King…oh…that reminds me, he gave me something for you," Zoltaire said getting up; walking to his waist belt he retrieved a sealed letter from his bag and swiftly delivered to Larian's hand.

"Ah, thank you," Larian said as Zoltaire sat back down.

"Anyway, I was just getting ready to leave when the marauders arrived. Those nobles did not look very noble!"

"I'm sure," Larian grimaced.

"I waited to see what would happen, and after they'd been taken away, the nobles, I mean, a cart packed with food and bowls, clothing, many things, was handed over to Zanock, and then the very best thing happened."

"What?"

"The King's own medicine man came out and left with them to tend to the leader's son."

"That is excellent news."

"The King looked much better when I left than when I arrived," Zoltaire said solemnly.

"Thank you for bringing me all this so speedily. It is all very good to hear."

"He said your meeting with Zanock was no accident, that it was the God's doing for many reasons."

"Maybe he's right," Larian sighed.

"I believe I will take myself to the warrior's house," Zoltaire announced, "unless there is more you need from me?"

"No, nothing. Take what foods you want with you. I have some thinking to do outside of all this, and I must do it before the East sun rises."

"Until we leave tomorrow then," Zoltaire said standing up.

"Yes, until then."

Taking his goblet of wine with him Larian ambled back to Lizbett's chamber, and silently entering he sat at a table in the corner of the room. Sipping his wine, gazing at his wife-to-be sleeping softly in her bed, he turned up the oil lamp, broke the seal on the letter and unfolded the paper.

Larian

The tale of your encounter with the marauders does not surprise me. Your skills as a warrior are not your only gifts, and though you are still young, you have an uncanny ability to see past the obvious, to be empathetic, to touch hearts and read minds. Should your wedding to Lizbett come to pass I would like to offer you the position of Head Negotiator of Verdana. You know this is a very influential post, and while some may see your youth as a disadvantage, I see it as just the opposite. I believe our adversaries will underestimate you, giving you the upper hand. (Of course I would offer this irrespective of the marriage, but I doubt your Prince would let you go).

I thank you most deeply, Larian, for all you have done for myself and my realm, and of course, for Lizbett. These are difficult days, and while I miss her very much it is best she is not here to witness the tumult that surrounds us.

Please give her my love, and I wait your response.

King Herandah of Verdana

Leaning back in his chair Larian took a deep breath.

Head Negotiator! I would be the King's right-hand man. This is astonishing.

Folding the letter he placed it on the table and stared across the room.

Lizbett. What a future we could have. It all rests on my shoulders now, my shoulders and your heart. I will do my best to win you, I will do my best to open the door, but it will be you who must step through it.

Picking up the letter he returned to his room, placed it carefully in his bag, then headed back to sit at Lizbett's side. Pulling up a chair he sat watching her sleep, pondering what he would do, what he would say and how he would say it.

She was wily indeed, and it was a trait she would need one day as Queen, if she really did want to control him they were doomed, but if she chose to surrender to him, to their love, then soon they would be sharing the glory of a life together.

He felt his eyes grow heavy; this was a good sign, this meant his mind was working and he would open them with answers. It was how he found his path outside of Zinyana. His small naps weren't exactly naps, but a closing of his controlling thoughts just enough to allow his inner guide to take over and show him the path.

It was the tweeting of a bird on the windowsill that stirred him. WIth his sensitive hearing it was as if it were sitting on his shoulder singing into his ear. Blinking open his eyes he stared out the window and saw the light of the East sun. Soon the household would stir, the morning meal would be laid out in the dining hall, and they would be leaving.

He realized his head felt clear. There was no worry or debate, and looking across at her he suddenly saw the map, what to say and what to do. Standing up and stretching he sat on the edge of the bed and touched her shoulder; she mumbled something, then frowned, then rolled on to her back and yawned.

"Good morning, Lizbett."

Her violet eyes fluttered open and she stared up at him.

"Mmm, what a wonderful sight. My warrior."

It brought a smile to his lips, and in that moment he could almost understand why her father had been so lenient. He could imagine her as a little girl, all eyes and hair, staring up at him innocently...*I'm sorry Pappa, I didn't mean it.* The vision was so clear he wondered if he'd once actually seen it, but of course he hadn't, and shutting it out of his mind he set about untying her wrists.

"Did you sleep well?" he asked.

"So well, even if my bottom is still sore and my nugget is starving."

Laying down next to her he pulled her into his arms inhaling the fragrance of her hair, and relishing the soft yielding of her body.

"I love this," she sighed, "being in your arms this way."

"Soon it will be every morning," he promised.

"It will?"

"I have decided our wedding should be soon, very soon, and I have also decided it should take place at my new home, with the blessing of your father and my Prince of course."

"Your home? I thought we would have a big celebration in the castle."

"I believe your father will be concerned about security at such an event, and the same is true with Zanderone, but at my residence it will be much safer. We can avoid the throngs that will arrive in either realm to mark the occasion, and enjoy the intimacy of a small number of invited guests."

He waited, praying that she would understand the ceremony was about the two of them, not just a time for adulation over her dress, her hair, and her warrior husband. This was the first thing he needed to hear, the first and most important.

"Larian, as I think upon it, I believe it will be even better," she said softly.

"Because?"

"Because it will be so special, and what better place to start our life than at your new home."

The surge of relief that traveled through his heart made him hug her tightly, squeezing her against his chest.

"Larian!"

"I must hold you this way for a moment," he said tenderly, "I must."

Her heart was true; it was her intense desire for boundaries, discipline and love that had sent her off course, and he knew exactly how to redirect it.

CHAPTER TWENTY-TWO

Much to Lizbett's delight the morning meal was served on the outside patio, and as she drank the honey tea, and ate the warm bread fresh from the oven smothered in vegetables that had been basted and baked until soft and creamy, she ooh'd and aah'd with every mouthful.

"Uncle, this is better than the food at the castle. Why does it taste so delicious?"

"It's the soil here," he smiled. "The fruits are sweeter, the vegetables have more flavor, even the milk and cheese from our animals has a richer taste and creamier texture."

"May I please buy some and have it delivered to father? He would enjoy it so much, and I would love to surprise him."

"For sale, no, to gift, yes, and it will be my honor to send him some as a token of our long friendship," Uncle replied. "Soon you will be my niece, and perhaps, if Larian honors you as he should, I will supply some tasty morsels for your wedding."

Larian knew exactly what his uncle meant; before breakfast Larian had taken him aside and told him of his epiphany during the night.

"As I thought," his uncle had nodded. "I could see it in her eyes. Do you know what to do?"

"I believe so, Uncle," Larian had replied.

"Then don't wait, do it with haste."

Selecting a slice of seeded bread from the basket in the center of the table, Larian covered it with soft cheese and smiled at him.

"Uncle, I can assure you, Lizbett will have all the honor she can handle."

"Honor? What is this talk of honor?" Lizbett frowned.

"Giving you honor by showing you affection," Larian replied, "and by teaching, by protecting and nurturing you."

"That sounds nice," she smiled.

"Now I must tell you the news Zoltaire brought from your father," Larian said soberly.

"Oh, my goodness, yes, tell us," she said eagerly.

As he relayed the report he saw his uncle take it all in, weighing the information and looking at it from different angles. When their meal came to an end, and Lizbett left to collect her things for the journey, his uncle gestured for him to remain behind.

"There's more," his uncle said knowingly.

"There is, Uncle," Larian said excitedly. "When I marry Lizbett the King wishes to appoint me as Head Negotiator."

"Hmmm, such an important post," his uncle remarked with a grave expression.

"You seem…unsure. I thought you'd be eager for me to have such an opportunity."

"Let me guess," his uncle began. "He says your youth is an advantage because his enemies, or those he's trading with, will underestimate you."

"Yes! Those are almost his exact words."

"He is right, but you are not just a young man, you are a Warrior Of The First Order. This tells your opponents you are exceptional, so the advantage of your youth is perhaps, overstated."

"Uncle, I don't understand your hesitation."

"If you accept this post you will be working directly with the King. If there are winning moments he will take most of the glory, in defeat you will bear the fault, and remember, Larian, being the King's Negotiator means travel and sitting across a table. I doubt you can be effective as both a Commander and a Negotiator. I suspect you would have to pick one or the other."

"I hadn't considered that," he pondered. "You think I should not accept?"

"I think we should discuss this further; those are just some thoughts to consider. You are the Kingdom's hero at the moment. Enjoy it for a while, make things right with Lizbett, have your wedding, then see how you feel. This situation, this offer, it has no time limit. You don't need to make such an important decision immediately; it is your youth that propels you forward with some impatience."

Larian stared into the man's eyes and shook his head.

"Uncle, I treasure your wisdom."

"It is only the advice of an old man, but I will always be here to offer it…at least until the Commander in the heavens calls me home."

"He can't. Your wisdom is too important to me."

"I believe he won't until you no longer need my counsel," his uncle murmured. "Now go, collect your things, your home is waiting, and more importantly, Lizbett is in need. Put her first and everything else will fall into place."

Larian hugged him, and as he did he could feel the solid muscles beneath the weathered skin. As he left and walked down the hallway to his room, he found solace in the powerful body he knew lived under his uncle's clothes.

I must have you in my life, Uncle, and I will for some time yet. You may carry many battle scars, but your body and mind are still strong.

A short time later the carriage and its retinue of warriors were rolling down the narrow lane away from the courtyard. Sitting across from her, Larian thought Lizbett appeared happy and rested; she had certainly been delighted when he'd told her he was going to share the first half of the journey with her.

"I think we should close the shades," she giggled as they reached the end of the lane and turned on to the road.

"The day is so bright, the scenery so interesting. You've never been here before. Don't you want to enjoy the new sights?"

"I'd rather be in your lap," she sighed, her violet eyes begging him for attention.

Ignoring her pleading request he let the silence tick for a while, then moved across and sat next to her.

"Does this mean I can draw the shades?" she twinkled.

"No, I want to talk to you," he said warmly, taking her hand and squeezing her fingers. "Tell me, when you were growing up and did something naughty, how would your mother or father punish you, or the woman who cared for you when they were busy?"

She stared back at him, surprise crossing her face, and he saw her happy expression began to dissolve.

"What do you mean?"

"It's not a difficult question," he said calmly.

"I'd rather talk about the question you put to me last night," she said with a slight edge to her voice.

"Hmm, well, with that question there is nothing to discuss, once you have the answer you will tell me," *but you won't have it, not yet. You won't have it until we pass through this difficult time.* "When you were a bad girl, how were you punished? Did you get your bottom smacked, were you locked in your room?"

"I don't want to talk about this," she scowled. "It doesn't matter."

"Your father told me a story about how he had once done that, locked you in your room. He said you climbed out a window. Is it true? Did you walk along the castle roof?"

"Why are we talking about this?" she said tersely. "I don't wish to go back to those days."

"Why not? Why is this upsetting you?"

"It's not upsetting me. It's just...I was...I am...I have my own mind about things, that's all."

"What happened when they discovered you had escaped through your window? What happened when they found you? Your father must have been very angry that you'd gone to such lengths to disobey him."

"Of course he was, what do you think?" she snapped.

He paused, and tilting his head to the side he frowned at her.

"Don't you think it's unwise to take that tone with me?"

She looked at him, dropped her eyes, and lifted his hand to her lips.

"I'm sorry, Larian. You're right. You should spank me for being so rude."

"Um, no, I don't think so," he said casually, then reaching into the bag on his waist belt he retrieved a piece of paper and a writing implement and scribbled something.

"What are you doing?" she asked.

"Just making a note."

"What kind of a note."

"You'll find out when I'm ready to tell you."

"But I want to know now!" she said vehemently.

"Oh, dear," he sighed scribbling again.

"Larian, this is most disconcerting. I insist, please, you must tell me what you're writing," she demanded.

"Why must I?"

"Because I want you to."

"I have already explained, Lizbett, you will not always get what you want with me."

"This isn't fair," she exclaimed, and to his astonishment she stamped her foot.

"What was that?" he asked, breaking into a grin.

"Now you're mocking me."

"I've just never seen anyone, except a tiny child of course, stamp their foot. It was amusing."

"Well, I'm not amused, I can tell you that!" she snapped.

"No, that's obvious, and you're not being very pleasant company either. Why won't you tell me about what happened after you climbed on to the roof?"

"Because there's nothing to tell, nothing happened, nothing at all," she exclaimed, almost shouting.

"And did that make you angry or happy?"

"Why are you interrogating me? Happy of course, and things got much better after that. I did as I pleased. Nothing happened about anything. Everyone was afraid I'd climb on to the roof again so they never locked me anywhere ever again," she declared triumphantly.

"Lizbett…there's something I must tell you."

"Why do you look so serious?"

"This is a serious matter, and I must have your complete attention."

"You're scaring me, and this is a strange conversation, all of it, the writing on that paper, everything," she frowned.

"I will no longer be spanking you, or punishing you, when you misbehave."

He stared at the look of shock crossing her face; it was a profound statement, and he knew it had shaken her.

"I…uh…why not?"

"Because, Lizbett, I can no longer allow you to control things, to control me. I know exactly what you've been doing, and it's coming to an end, right now, right this minute."

He saw the deep crimson blush start at her neck, and slowly crawl up and over her face.

"What…uh…I…don't know what you mean," she stammered.

"Oops, that was a lie," he mumbled, and opened the piece of paper to scribble yet again.

"Larian, please," she begged, her eyes brimming with tears, "please tell me what's going on, the questions, that paper…"

"I will, but only if you tell me the truth," he said, his aqua eyes sizzling across at her.

She stared back at him, but only for a minute, then dropping her gaze, in a very tiny voice she said,

"You're right," she quivered. "I have, uh, been bad so you would, uh, punish me," and burst into tears.

CHAPTER TWENTY-THREE

He held her and rocked her and let her cry. They were the first tears he'd seen her shed and it broke his heart, but he knew they were good tears, cleansing tears, tears of frustration finally being released. When they began to abate she pulled back to wipe her face, and when he looked into her eyes they were no longer deep violet, but soft mauve.

"What is it?" she asked seeing the bewilderment on his face.

"It's your eyes."

"What about them?"

"They're lighter, much lighter."

"They...they are?" she managed still composing herself. "I don't understand. How strange. There were times when I was much younger that they were lighter."

"That's extraordinary," Larian exclaimed.

"Do they look...okay?"

"They look beautiful," he smiled. "You look beautiful."

"I wish there was a reflecting glass here."

"They're beautiful, truly," he assured her.

She sighed and kissed his neck, then laid her head back on his shoulder.

"When was the last time you cried, Lizbett?"

"Um...a long time ago. When you left the stables."

"Not since then?"

"No. There were times I felt it but I pushed it away."

"Poor Lizbett," he crooned stroking her hair.

"Please will you tell me what you meant about not punishing me anymore?" she softly asked.

"I didn't say that. I said I'm no longer going to punish you at the time you misbehave. I'm going to do things differently from now on."

"How?"

"I'll tell you the new rules," he said firmly, "but first I must explain something. When you were growing up it was confusing when you weren't punished for being a bad girl, so you did even worse things trying to get the attention you wanted. Still nothing happened and it was very upsetting for you. Does that sound right?"

"It does, it does," she said urgently. "I felt like nobody cared."

"They cared, they cared very much, but you had a stronger will. They didn't know what to do so they gave up. You won a battle you didn't want to win."

"You're right," she whispered.

"You don't just have a strong will, you're very clever, and one day those things will make you a great Queen, not to mention a formidable opponent, but I will tell you, Lizbett, and this is for certain, your will, it is not stronger than mine, and your clever brain, mine will outwit yours every time."

She stared back at him, feeling her heart thump in her chest, and the flippity flip spring to life.

"I can sense it," she murmured, "I think I must have sensed it all those years ago. Thank the Gods you came to that stable back then. Thank the Gods."

Lifting her mouth to meet his she kissed him with a woman's passion, moving her lips and tongue, lightly biting and nibbling, then breaking away she sank into his chest.

"I ache to lay with you," she breathed, "and now I feel worthy of it."

Engulfing her, his powerful arms wrapping her up, he closed his eyes and felt the new softness of her being.

"You always have been worthy," he murmured, "but now you are learning who Lizbett is, you are learning who I am."

They nestled for a while, feeling the shroud of their new intimacy, then Larian pushed her back.

"From now on," he said firmly, "you will not be punished at the time you do something wrong, but I will make a note of it, and once a week you will receive whatever punishment I deem necessary for your naughty deeds."

"That sounds...kind of scary," she stammered. "I mean, adding it up like that."

"In addition I will spank you every morning. It will be short and sharp. I have decided that a spanking a day will keep the petulance away."

"Every morning?"

"Yes, every morning," he repeated, "until I decide otherwise. If you're very bad I won't spank you at all, but I will keep your nugget starving for a long time."

"Sir," she breathed.

"Lastly, if I ever, and I do mean ever, sense that you are attempting to control me or manipulate me, I will have to assume you no longer desire my company."

"I will always desire you," she said solemnly.

"Do you understand everything I've told you?"

"Yes, I do, everything," she nodded, and the look in her mauve eyes told him she did; it was slightly apprehensive, but filled with love and respect.

"The day we met up at the bridge and I spanked you at the waterfall, you finally got what you'd been craving, but your hunger for it was so strong you went to great lengths to get more of it."

"It's true, Larian, I'm so sorry," she apologized as the red blush returned. "I didn't know how else to...you know...get you to do that."

"Those days are over. You will be subject to my discipline as I see fit, and there will be times you will disagree, but that's not going to change my mind."

"I want this," she said softly. "I want this very much."

"I know," he smiled. "Now tell me, how is your nugget, wife-to-be?"

"My nugget?" she smiled. "My nugget is hungrier than ever."

"I think I'd like to check," he murmured. "Close the shades."

Sighing happily she kissed him lightly, then moved around the carriage pulling the thick red fabric over the windows. Returning the paper to his bag he felt his heart fill with relief and joy; she would still be difficult, but he believed his uncle's last words; everything would fall into place.

"Pull up your dress and petticoats, untie the cord that holds up your underthings, and stretch over my lap," he said as she hurried back to him.

"What?"

"I'm not going to spank you, Lizbett, just do as I say. Head and legs on the seat. I want you to be comfortable."

Gathering up the many folds of material, she undid the knot allowing her underwear to drop, then laid herself out, wriggling over his thighs so her body was as he'd instructed.

"How do you feel?"

"Happy," she sighed. "I like it here."

"I know that," he grinned staring at her splotchy round cheeks, "and you will find yourself in this position a great deal, both for pleasure and for punishment. I will begin your morning spanking after two passages of the moon. It will give your beautiful bottom time to fully recover, but now...now I will make your nugget very happy."

She let out a grateful moan, and moving his fingers into her slit he found her delightfully wet. Touching where his cock would soon penetrate he pushed forward, and like a flower greeting the rise of the East sun, she spread her legs and her channel opened, inviting his fingers to enter.

164

"I know you have not laid with a man," he murmured pushing his finger forward, "yet I find no…"

"No, of course not," she interrupted. "I've never wanted any man to even kiss me, not any man except you."

"It is because you have been riding astride a horse for so long. That is the cause. It has worn away the thin membrane that allows a man to know you are still a maiden."

"Oh, no, is that bad?" she asked turning her head to stare at him over her shoulder.

"No, it will make your first time much easier, there should be no pain," he reassured her, and as he slid his finger further forward she let out a little cry, then laid her head back down.

"Does this feel nice to you?" he asked softly.

"So nice, so very nice. It makes me want more, it makes me tingle, oh, Larian, it makes me feel many things."

"I will do this a great deal before our wedding night, so when my mighty cock thrusts for the first time you will feel only pleasure, much pleasure," he crooned.

Dropping his thumb against her tiny, sensitive nub he pressed and circled, then paused to move his finger in and out. She gasped and moaned and wriggled, and as the carriage carried them forward he continued the dance; stirring her nugget, then pumping his finger, alternating between the two, bringing her higher and higher, until she wailed her bliss.

"Larian, it's upon me, it's upon me!"

"Let it flow," he exclaimed, and resting his finger in her cunt he vigorously rubbed this thumb over her swollen kernel.

She gasped, her body stiffened, and the spasm hit. Her head snapped back, and her shrill cries filled the small cabin; he milked her moment, never pausing his attention, until her yowls finally abated and she fell limp. Removing his hand he caressed her bottom for a moment, then pulled her up to curl into his body.

"Larian," she panted, "I have no words. I feel fresh tears."

"You don't need words," he sighed, "when the feeling is so strong there are none."

Though his cock was pulsing, all thought was on her; moments passed, then she raised her beautifully flushed face, and her soft mauve eyes sparkled at him.

"I can feel your rod," she said coyly. "It needs to do that too."

"It does," he smiled.

"Do you want me to use my hand as I did before?"

"I would like that very much, but in future you will say, please may I have the honor of pleasing your cock, and I will say, yes or no. Then I will tell you if you should use your hand or your mouth."

"My mouth?" she gasped.

"Don't fret, Lizbett, I will teach you, but after our wedding. I mention it now because you must think about it, consider it, dream about what joy it will bring you."

"My goodness, the thought quite takes my breath away."

"And doing it probably will too," he smiled, "but for now you must say the words. Do you remember them?"

"Please may I have the honor of pleasing your cock?" she asked timidly.

"Yes, with your hand."

"Thank you, Sir."

"Good girl," he murmured stroking her hair.

"It makes me so happy when you say that," she sighed. "It positively fills me."

He smiled, then kissed her, showing his approval with his warm, loving, moist lips.

"Now," he said pulling back, "now you may pleasure my cock. It is eager to feel your delicate fingers."

She slipped from his lap to sit beside him, but he moved her on to her knees.

"This is the position you will take when you do this," he said firmly.

"Yes, Sir, I will remember."

Opening the wooden buttons, she pulled down the flap and found his stiffened cock already oozing tiny, clear drops. She gazed at it for a moment, then wrapping her fingers around the thick shaft she began to stroke, moving her hand up and down in a strong, consistent rhythm.

"Yes, that's it, good girl, just like that," he muttered staring down at her, then resting his head back he closed his eyes to sink into the delightfully satisfying sensation.

As he sensed his moment brewing he surrendered to the gentle rocking of the carriage as it joined with her artful attention, allowing the buildup to take its course. He had been well-trained and had control of his eruption, but he decided to allow nature to dictate his release, and for the first time in many moons he exerted no self-control.

It was a marvelous thing…to simply allow it to happen of its own accord…and when it did, when the explosion jerked his cock, he felt the powerful moment surge through his body.

The climax was deep and fierce, the convulsions rippling through him sending shockwaves of sparks, and when the intoxicating moment was finally done with him, and she was tenderly wiping him with her petticoats, he opened his eyes to a thousand tiny lights. He'd experienced the moment hundreds of times, but it was unlike any that had come before.

Utterly drained he barely felt her put him away, replace the flap and settle back beside him.

"Larian, are you all right?" she whispered.

Barely finding the strength, he lifted his arm and pulled her into his shoulder.

"No, I'm much better than all right," he mumbled, *and I just learned how a small woman can bring a mighty warrior to his knees.*

CHAPTER TWENTY-FOUR

They slept. It wasn't planned and neither had suggested it; it just happened. The gentle rolling ride lulled them as they drifted, and when Larian was woken by a gentle knock on the carriage door his eyes bolted open.

He was startled that he had napped so peacefully; it was rare for a warrior to simply drift away, and shaking his head he gently pulled his arm from around Lizbett's body, still curled into him, and moved to the door.

"Commander, we are very close to your house."

It was Zoltaire, and he knew Larian would not wish to arrive at his residence in a carriage.

"So soon?" Larian frowned.

"We have traveled through the passage of the moons," Zoltaire replied. "The East sun has just risen."

Stunned by the news he looked past Zoltaire into the distance, then raised his eyes to the sky.

Zoltaire is right. How can it be? This is astonishing.

"Thank you," he mumbled. "Please bring Thunder but without his saddle. I shall ride with Lizbett. We shall approach together."

"Yes, Commander."

Closing the door he turned around to see Lizbett stretching her arms above her head; her eyes were closed, and when she opened them she spotted her undergarments still laying on the floor. Hastily jumping from her seat she snatched them up and attempted to pull them up, but she lost her balance and fell backwards, landing on the cushions she'd just been sitting on. Larian burst into laughter.

"This isn't funny," she exclaimed struggling to pull them up amidst her billowing petticoats.

"Do you need help?" he asked unable to suppress his laughter.

"No, yes, no," she stammered, then unable to stop herself began giggling hysterically.

"I think you do," he quipped.

Taking her by the arms he stood her up, then told her to hold up her many underclothes as he slid the underwear up her legs and tied off the knot.

"My goodness, what a lot of fluffy finery you must wear."

"It's too much. When I'm Queen I'm going change things," she declared. "I'm going to start new fashions for women. All of this is ridiculous."

"That will be an interesting time," he remarked as he smoothed her dress, "I think I'm going to enjoy that part of your reign."

"Why have we stopped?" she asked, suddenly realizing they weren't moving.

"We're very close, and Zoltaire knows I would not wish to arrive at my new residence in a carriage."

"Oh, so you're going to ride?"

"Yes, and so are you."

"But..I don't have a saddle, Scarlet might get excited."

"I think Scarlet will be too tired to be excited but it doesn't matter, I didn't mean you're going to ride Scarlet. You're going to sit on Thunder with me."

"I am?"

"You are. You and I will approach together. You will be seated as a lady should be, not astride, but with your legs over

169

one side mounted in front of me. Now help me pull the shades back."

Still thinking about his suggestion she helped open the shades, but when she spied Larian's big black horse through the window she paused, and looked at Larian with wary eyes.

"He's so tall and big. Will it be safe?"

"Thunder is a much safer horse than your Scarlet," he said soberly. "Don't you remember when we met at the bridge? I could see you were envious of how well behaved he was."

"I remember…it's just…he's so big," she repeated.

"Lizbett, I would not suggest it if I thought for even one moment there would be any risk. Once we are settled in our married life I will teach you how to ride properly," he promised, "and how to make Scarlet calmer and happier."

"Like me," she sighed.

"Yes, like you," he smiled. "Don't worry, I'll keep you safe. I will always keep you safe!"

Taking her hand he helped her from the carriage, but when she stood beside the towering horse she felt a ripple of fear. His back was high and wide, his mane was thick and flowing around him, and when his huge head turned and his brown eyes stared down at her she clutched Larian's sleeve.

"Are you sure?"

"Yes, be brave, trust me."

Then it struck him.

The Lizbett he'd met at the bridge the day he'd returned to Verdana would never have shown her fear; she would have either found an excuse not to get on, or pretended she had no problem at all and pushed past her worry to show she wasn't afraid of anything.

"Lizbett," he said softly, dropping his lips to her ear, "I'm very proud of you right now."

Startled, she turned and gazed up at him, and though she didn't understand why he was so happy with her, she saw the approval in his aqua eyes.

"Uh, thank you," she replied with a half-smile. "How am I supposed to get up there?"

"Zoltaire will lift you."

"Yes, Princess, from the step of the carriage," Zoltaire said climbing from his horse and moving forward.

With a move that astounded her, Larian grabbed a large chunk of his horse's mane, leapt from the ground and flipped his legs over Thunder's back while the horse remained completely still; Lizbett stared up in disbelief.

"How did you do that?"

"Practice," he laughed. "Your turn."

Walking nervously back to the carriage she climbed up on the step, and taking her by the waist Zoltaire lifted her easily into Larian's waiting arms.

"Ooh, it's so high up here," she exclaimed.

"Sit back against my chest," Larian said as he put his arms protectively around her and picked up the reins. "Relax, you're stiff, just relax and settle in. Thunder won't move until I ask him to."

Taking a deep breath Lizbett shifted her seat until she found a spot that felt comfortable, then sank into the horse's back, and leaned into Larian's chest.

"There, feel better?"

"Much, wow," she smiled, "this is kind of fun."

Larian laughed, delighted with her, and asked Thunder to move slowly forward.

"I love this," she squealed, reminding Larian that while she was a woman full of passion, there remained inside her a young, exuberant girl.

The caravan picked up the pace, and though remaining at a walk for Lizbett's confidence and comfort they were soon turning into the drive leading to Larian's house.

"Larian," she breathed, "it's beautiful."

A two-story pale yellow home stood impressively at the end of the drive. Gardeners were attending a row of flowering bushes that sat on either side of the steps leading to the front door; white shutters framed the windows, and several chimneys told her there were many fireplaces.

As they drew closer she spied a matching stable to the side of the house, with large fenced paddocks, then moving her eyes to the opposite side she spied a wide terrace with white balustrades, and large, round white pots with trailing blooms.

"It's just beautiful," she repeated.

"It's not a castle," Larian remarked.

"No, it's not a castle, it's a home, it's a beautiful home, a real home."

He could hear a crack in her voice, and he understood.

"It will be our home," he whispered in her ear. "The castle will be our place of work, but this will be our home."

The warriors went directly to the stables, but Zoltaire followed Larian to the front steps and quickly dismounted, then stood next to Thunder ready to catch Lizbett as Larian helped her slide off.

"It's so far," she bleated staring down at Zoltaire waiting arms.

"You ran across a castle roof," Larian reminded her.

"But that was different."

"You can't stay up here all day. Just let yourself slide. Zoltaire will catch you. Either that or I'll get off first and you can-"

"NO! Sorry, no, please don't go anywhere. All right, here I go. Are you ready, Zoltaire?"

"Yes, Princess, I've done this before, I'm ready."

Larian moved his arms from around her and placed his hands at her waist to help her balance, then putting her hands behind her she gave herself a gentle push; the slide was easy, and as promised Zoltaire caught her as though she weighed no more than a leaf falling from a tree.

"Thank you," she sighed grinning up at him.

"My pleasure, Princess," he smiled back.

A moment later Larian flipped off his horse and handed him over to Zoltaire.

"I'll have food brought to the warrior's house right away," Larian said, "and in my report to our Prince I'll make sure he knows all you did."

"Thank you, Commander," he said with a slight nod, and Lizbett saw how proud he was to have received Larian's approval.

I know how he feels. That's what I want, Larian's approval, I want to please him.

Like the lightening bolt of Larian's epiphany, the revelation sparked through her.

"Larian, I must speak to you, in private, it's important," she said urgently.

"Then we will go into the house," he replied. "Are you all right?"

"Yes, I'm very all right," she smiled, her soft mauve eyes twinkling up at him.

"I'll see you soon, Zoltaire, and thank you. Please give the men my praise."

Taking her by the elbow he walked her up the steps, acknowledging the gardeners as he did, complimenting them on how attractive the bushes appeared, and how the landscaping was even more appealing than when he'd left; again Lizbett saw how they glowed under his favor.

He opened the door, and Lizbett didn't take even a moment to glance around the foyer, but clutched his hands.

"I have the answer," she beamed.

"The answer?"

"To your question. More than anything else, what makes me happy?"

Larian felt his pulse quicken and he took a quick breath.

"What is it?"

"Pleasing you. More than anything else, pleasing you…that will make me happier than anything."

Letting out a deep, gratified sigh, Larian pulled her into his body.

"Thank you, Lizbett, that is the answer I was seeking. You've made me very happy."

CHAPTER TWENTY-FIVE

L arian gave her the tour of his house and Lizbett fell in love with everything she saw, but there were rooms that were empty, still waiting to be furnished.

"I have some things in my apartment that would be wonderful here," she gushed, "and I can have the royal furniture-makers custom design some pieces just for us."

"I love your enthusiasm to make this home just right," he smiled, "but it will be done on my coin. The castle belongs to the Kingdom, it is the heart of the realm and it must be a certain way, but this home of ours, it will be comfortable and inviting, and when little children are running around they must not fear breaking something valuable."

"Little children?" she breathed.

"Little children, puppies, us," he grinned.

A warm fuzzy feeling moved through her body, and she rose on to her toes and pecked him on the cheek.

"You're right," she agreed, "but I can bring special, personal things, can't I?"

"Of course, but we will select our furniture together, both of us...together," he repeated staring at her with a look that said he meant it.

"Yes, Sir," she winked with a cheeky grin.

A large feast had been readied in preparation for Larian's return, and when they moved into the dining hall to sit down for their meal, the cook, the kitchen helper and the general housekeeper were waiting for them. Larian made the introductions, informed them that Princess Lizbett would be his bride, and that the wedding arrangements would be quickly made.

"I don't know if the ceremony will take place here or in Zanderone, but you will know very soon."

The small staff were overjoyed, and curtsied and congratulated them, then hurried away so they could begin to serve the meal.

"There are a few things you should know," Larian began as he poured some freshly squeezed juice from an exotic fruit Lizbett had not seen before. "When I enter the sleep of Zinyana you may lay next to me, but you cannot lay on top of any of my limbs. I believe I made that clear to you before, but it bears repeating."

"Yes, of course," she said solemnly. "I'll never forget what happened to your arm."

"You cannot disturb me. If someone comes to the door to see me they must wait. The staff here understands that, and you must too."

"What if it's some kind of emergency."

"Only, and I repeat, only, in a very dire emergency you may whisper my name and gently touch my shoulder, then leave. I must bring myself up slowly, and it is better I am alone to do this."

"How often do you go into Zinyana?"

"Every three days, but it does depend on what's happening. Even though I had that sleep in the carriage, I can feel my body is asking to be restored so I must do it tonight. Until our wedding night you will be sleeping in the guest quarters so there won't be any problem, unless you decide to be naughty as you were in the castle."

"No, I won't," she promised.

"Tomorrow I will show you the boundaries of my land, and Lizbett, you must not go beyond them. You are completely safe here; it is known this land belongs to a Warrior Of The First Order, and a Commander, and that there is a retinue of guards that live here, so no-one would dare attempt to break in, but outside there are regular people and that means not all of them are good."

"I don't want to go anywhere without you, Larian, so you don't have to worry."

"Excuse me, Sir."

Larian looked up and saw the housekeeper holding a sealed letter.

"This just arrived," she said walking over to him. "The messenger is waiting for a response."

"Tell the messenger I'll be with him shortly. Please be sure he receives something to drink and eat if he desires it."

"Yes, Sir."

Lizbett watched him break the seal and unfold the paper, then smile.

"What is it?" she asked eager to hear the good news.

"It's from my Prince. All is stable in Zanderone. The attempted takeover of the throne appears to have been limited to Verdana, but he understands the safety concerns for you so he gives his blessing should we choose to have our wedding ceremony here."

"How did he find out about us so fast?"

"A warrior cannot marry without permission from his Prince," Larian said solemnly, "and he knew my reason for visiting Verdana."

"You knew you wanted me before you left Zanderone?"

"I told you that."

"Well, yes…but I wasn't…I mean I didn't know you'd been so sure."

"A warrior is always prepared. Better to ask permission and not need it, than have to wait for it to be granted."

"Oh, yes, that makes sense," she said slowly.

"Plus, I'm sure your father told him I was bringing you back here with me when he sent his own message the night of the banquet. It's not advanced battlefield training to figure out what was happening between us."

"So…we have father's blessings, and the Prince's."

"We do, and you want to know-"

"-if tomorrow after the West sun rises is too soon for our ceremony," she interrupted with a wide smile

"Um, yes," he laughed. "I would suggest ten passes of the moons. That will give us time to prepare the house, determine who will attend and send their notices-"

"-and for me to have the dress made, but wait, I know exactly what I will wear, but I need a handmaiden, someone trustworthy, and I don't want the servant I had at the castle. She was a dull girl."

"I have an idea," he said. "Falayla. She saved your life, she saved all our lives, and that would be a fitting reward."

"Didn't she…uh…flirt with you in the banquet ante-chamber," Lizbett frowned, "and that reminds me, why did Zoltaire say he'd helped ladies off Thunder before?"

"Lizbett, do you think you are the only woman who has felt the touch of my lips or the caress and sting of my hand?" he asked incredulous at her question

"I don't like to think about it," she pouted.

"Where is my bag," he muttered, and pulling it from his waist belt he retrieved the piece of paper and his writing implement.

"What are you doing? I was only asking a question," she protested.

"No, you were being jealous and insecure, and I believe you were beginning to pout," he declared as he scribbled.

"I don't like this new way of discipline at all," she quipped.

"Do you wish me to send a message to Falayla or not?" he asked ignoring her comment.

"Do you want me to?"

"It matters not to me. I simply suggested her because I think she deserves it."

"It would be good if I did use her, wouldn't it?" she mumbled.

"Yes, it would be good, but you should only have a girl you really want, otherwise you won't be happy."

"I shall think on it today, and give you my answer before you enter Zinyana."

"That will be fine," he smiled, "and I shall respond to the Prince's message that the ceremony will take place here, ten passes of the moon from tonight."

"Larian, I'm so excited, so very, very excited."

"The messenger is waiting so I must write the note. Continue your meal. I'll return in a moment."

She watched him leave, and as she considered his suggestion of using Falayla as her servant, she stared out the window at the grounds beyond and her mind began to wander.

What a journey this has been. I wonder why he didn't want me to bring any fine clothes. I suppose I shall know soon enough. Clothes, my goodness I must unpack, and I ache for a soak. I hope there's a tub here, I didn't check any of the anti-rooms.

A short time later the housekeeper bustled back in with a fresh plate of baked fowl, and after placing it on the table she curtsied and looked at Lizbett expectantly.

"Excuse me, Princess."

"Yes?"

"The Commander asked me to tell you that he has been called to the warrior's house and might be a while."

"Oh, um, thank you. Tell me, is there a soaking tub here?"

"Yes, Princess, in the Commander's anteroom."

"But not in the guest chamber."

"No, Princess."

"Would you please fill the soaking tub with warm water and rose petals."

"Of course, Princess, I shall see to it at once, but we don't have rose petals here. We do have another fragrant flower, it is similar."

"That will be fine, just something nicely scented to rid me of this smell of travel."

"I will see to it at once, Princess," she said, then curtsied again and hurried away.

Lizbett realized she didn't know the formalities of Zanderone. In Verdana it wasn't necessary for the servants to continually curtsy, just once, the first time of the day, and she made a mental note to ask Larian how she should behave around his Prince and his court.

She continued her meal, ate some of the baked fowl and found it to her liking, drank some of the honey flavored drink that had been served in a large carafe, then leaned back in her chair and sighed.

He's taking so long. I hope there is nothing wrong with his men. I'm dying for a soak. I think I'll just go ahead. Hopefully by the time I'm finished and dressed he'll be back.

Rising from her chair she made her way up the stairs, entered his bed chamber, and found the housekeeper leaving the anteroom; as before the woman immediately curtsied.

"The soaking tub is filled with warm water and the fragrant petals from the flower rosamine," she declared. "I hope it is to your liking."

"Thank you, please see I'm not disturbed."

"Of course, Princess," the housekeeper replied, and curtsied again.

"That could get really annoying," Lizbett muttered as she entered the anteroom and closed the door.

Peeling off her clothes she stepped carefully into the tub and sank into the warm, inviting water; it was the largest tub she'd ever been in, and she realized it had to be oversized to accommodate Larian's tall, wide frame. The aroma of the petals filled her sensitive nostrils, and she new immediately it was a combination of rose and jasmine.

How did they bring the two together? How extraordinary. I would love to see the flower.

Stretching out and laying back she closed her eyes. She was so happy, as happy as she'd ever been, and though the skin on her bottom was still tender she didn't mind a bit; on the contrary she liked the feeling.

The memory of the delicious, devouring explosion across Larian's lap inside the carriage began to float into her mind, and her hand wandered down her body and between her legs.

It was so amazing, I wonder if I can make it happen by myself. Maybe he released something inside me that has been preventing me from-

"No, Lizbett."

Her eyes shot open, and standing over her Larian looked bigger than life.

"Why not? You have not forbidden it."

"You're correct, it was my oversight," he smiled, and kneeling beside the tub he dropped his hand in the water. "This is a precious jewel," he purred as he moved his fingers into her slit and touched her nub, "and it belongs to me."

"Larian," she sighed, "it feels so wonderful when you do that, but it is my body. I don't understand why I can't touch it."

"Do you not belong to me?" he asked patiently.

"Uh, yes, but-"

"There is no but. Your luscious breasts," he continued, moving his fingers up to tweak her nipples, "they belong to me too, your bottom is mine to spank or caress as I choose, and this precious jewel," he purred moving his fingers back between her legs, "this most especially, is to be handled only by me."

"And if it is hungry?"

"You will tell me, and I will decide if it deserves to be fed."

"It is hungry now," she said softly. "Is there any reason it shouldn't be satisfied?"

"There is the list in my bag, but those items will be addressed in five more passes of the moons, so at the moment I see no reason it should not have the attention it craves."

"Do you mean that it will be left hungry because of the list?"

"If the list grows, I suspect it might," Larian replied raising his eyebrows.

"I don't like that list," she frowned.

"As you said earlier, but do you want to talk about the list, or do you want me to give your nugget what it wants?"

"Oh, definitely that," she said fervently.

"Are you almost finished with your soak?"

"I am, it was divine, I needed it so badly," she sighed.

"Then dry yourself off and I will be waiting on my bed."

"Thank you, Larian," she smiled. "Will you help me so I won't slip? This is such a large tub."

"Of course," he said, and gripping her upper arm he helped her to her feet, then added, "I think I shall soak for a moment myself while you dry off. Lock the chamber door and lay on my bed, hands above your head so you won't be tempted."

"Yes, Sir," she said reaching for a large absorbent cloth the housekeeper had left her.

"Wait," he said as he lowered himself down. "I'd rather you wait for me on your knees and elbows."

Lizbett paused, picturing how she would appear, and a hot blush began to cross her face.

"Sir?"

"Yes?"

"Did you say, knees and elbows?"

"I did, and your face in a pillow."

"But, uh…"

"Do I need to add to the list?"

"NO, no, Sir, I shall wait as you ask."

As she padded from the anteroom he broke into a smile.

The list. I am so glad it occurred to me. I must share it with Uncle next time I see him.

CHAPTER TWENTY-SIX

L izbett was mortified. She'd been waiting on her knees and elbows with her head buried in a pillow just as he'd instructed, but the thought of how she must look was burning her face.

Why does he want me like this? It's so...open. I'm so open. He'll see all of me in a very...open way.

"What a good girl you are."

She hadn't heard him approach, and while she found his praise comforting it wasn't enough to alleviate her hot embarrassment, but when his hand dropped underneath her torso to gently squeeze each of her breasts it helped, and as his soft caress continued she found herself thinking more about his warm, tantalizing fingers than her lewd pose.

"Is this position difficult for you?" he purred.

"Yes, very," she managed.

"But you did it anyway. That pleases me, Lizbett, I'm proud of you."

"Th...thank you."

"I didn't ask you to do this to make you uncomfortable, though I knew you would be. I asked you so you'd have an opportunity to please me in spite of how it felt, and you did. This makes me very happy."

She sighed, then moaned, and as he climbed on to the bed behind her she let out a small whimper.

"Yes, Lizbett, I can see all of you, and every part of you is beautiful."

Hearing another whimper he smoothed his palm over her backside. Its fading marks suggested the acute soreness had passed, but he assumed there'd be some residual tenderness. Placing his hands on her cheeks he fondled and gently pinched, bringing the blood to the surface, then traveling his hands to her legs he stroked her inner thighs, then squeezed her skin just enough to tantalize.

"Ooh, Sir."

"You are starting to feel better," he said softly, spying her tell-tale wetness.

"A bit," she whimpered.

Moving his hands to the pink folds he tenderly separated them and touched his finger to the entrance of her trough; he was rewarded with a bleating moan and a wriggle.

To view her charms in the light of day, completely naked and so utterly exposed sent his cock surging to attention, and taking it firmly in his hand he placed it where his finger had just touched.

"You are tight and small," he murmured. "I'll have to play with you each day so you will be ready for our first night as husband and wife."

"As you wish, Sir," she mewled, her voice muffled by the pillow.

"The sight of you, Lizbett, it takes my breath away. You are divine, absolutely divine."

Keeping his cock at her entrance he moved his fingers to her sweet nut and gently rubbed; she immediately turned her head to the side, gasping with delight.

"Thank you, thank you," she breathed, and wriggled again, dislodging his cock from its resting place.

Just as well. If she opened up it would be very difficult not to press home and she's not ready. I must work her.

"Lizbett, move your hand against your nugget. I want to see you rub it."

"You do? But I thought-"

"I'm instructing you to," he said continuing to massage it himself. "I will enjoy watching."

Lifting her hand she moved it underneath her body, and when her fingers touched his a spark of heat flooded her loins.

"Sir," she breathed, "to feel your fingers upon me and to touch them with mine, it makes me tingle."

"Massage, Lizbett, massage freely."

He watched her fingers circle and knead, and dropping the hand that had been fondling her cheek he began rubbing himself, but allowed the indulgence for only a few moments.

Shifting his focus back to his more important task he inserted his forefinger into her narrow, moist channel; though long and thick his finger fit her perfectly, and he began to frig her, rhythmically pushing it in and sliding it out

As he increased the tempo he saw that her fingers followed suit; she was moaning and wriggling, all thought of her salacious exposure having been swept away by her craving need. To his delight her slippery juices began to flow, and presenting a second finger he carefully pushed forward; her soaked trough opened and accepted, and feeling a rush through his loins he felt his cock wanting to burst.

"Oh, Lizbett," he growled, "you are such a passionate, hungry girl."

His words and the thickness of his two fingers thrusting into her channel sent a wash of energy coursing through her, and without thought she bucked her bottom, and unabashedly cried out her need.

"Please, Sir, do it harder, faster."

Quickly shifting to her side he wrapped his arm across her hips, and plunging his fingers forward he let caution fly and frigged aggressively.

"Yes, oh, I love it, I love it," she wailed.

"Head into the pillow, cry and scream if you must, but into the pillow," he said urgently, worried the servants might hear her.

"More," she whispered, "harder and more."

Overjoyed he pumped with hard, slow, forceful strokes, and a moment later he received his reward; she pushed back against his hand, released a low howl, and her walls pulsed against his fingers.

Quickening the thrusts he milked her moment, giving her as much pleasure as the climax could offer. She bucked and uttered her cries of joy as the spasms fired, until, with a last gasp, she dropped her hand from her sex and moaned her bliss. Slowly withdrawing his fingers, but keeping his arm around her hips, he fondled her bottom cheeks.

"Sir," she whimpered.

"Stay as you are," he said softly, "I love looking at you this way."

He smoothed his hand over her luscious curves as he stared at the saturated, bright pink flesh between her thighs, and gazed fondly at her most private part nestled between her proud, round cheeks, then slowly returned to his position directly behind her.

"I am going to erupt over your lovely bottom," he purred, "then we can both return to the soaking tub and wash each other."

"Mmm," she mumbled, still lost in the afterglow of her moment.

Gripping his cock he massaged fervently, admiring all she had to offer. He could almost feel the hot tightness of her trough, and wondered how he could wait ten passes of the moons before taking it. Gazing at her tight puckered hole he felt a surge of energy when he thought about how he would train her there, and that was his last thought before his life essence rose up and squirted over her cheeks. As he watched the cream dribble into her crack, he couldn't resist the temptation, and dropping his finger he lightly followed it, whispering across her tiny button.

She made a strange sound but didn't move, and taking it as a final, wonderful, encouraging moment, he fell beside her and opened his arms. Sighing happily, she lowered her body on to the bed and rolled on her side, pressing against him.

"We're both naked," she sighed.

"We are."

"Is that allowed before our wedding night?"

Sitting up slightly he looked around the room, then flopped back down.

"I don't see anyone here to arrest us," he said solemnly.

The comment sent her giggling and she covered her face with her hands, then dropped them away.

"You know what I mean."

"I am the Master of his house, and I am the Master of you and this glorious body of yours, so if I say it's allowed, then it's allowed. Plunging my cock into you though, that must wait."

"We've done everything else, why should we wait?"

"Oh, Princess, we certainly have not done everything else, not at all."

"Really?"

"Really, and some of it I'm saving."

"I don't think I can wait," she moaned.

"If I can wait, you can wait, and we both will. Are you ready to get back in the tub?"

"No, not yet. Can we lay here for just a few more minutes? I love being this way. I feel so close to you."

Sighing contentedly he closed his eyes and enveloped her.

"Larian, you were right about Falayla. Of course I should ask her. It was childish of me not to think so."

"Good girl," he purred, "you are growing up."

CHAPTER TWENTY-SEVEN

They had enjoyed a playful time in the large soaking tub, had taken a wander through the grounds, and it was just after their evening meal, when both suns had set and the moons were beginning their ascent, when Larian looked across the table at her and wearily announced he was retiring for a full night of Zinyana. Taking his arm Lizbett walked with him to the door of his bed chamber and leaned her head against his chest.

"How will I get through tonight alone, and the many nights ahead until our wedding?" she sighed.

"I believe, Lizbett, the time will be taken very quickly with all the preparations. Tomorrow we must send out the notices, so tonight you must make your list of those you wish to attend. Keep it very small, we cannot accommodate a large group, but when things are settled we can have a grand reception in Verdana if you would like it."

"I don't much care," she said honestly, "but I believe my father will require it."

"As will my Prince in Zanderone," he said. "I have my guest list in my head, so when I wake as the East sun rises I will send out the messengers. Leave your list in the drawer of my desk in case you're not yet awake."

"I just thought of something, where are we going to put father and mother? There are only two other bedrooms besides mine."

"Tomorrow we will go through all this. Rest assured the answers are there. Now I must restore my body. I can feel it is drained and my mind is weary."

"Goodnight, Larian. I shall be with you as you sleep."

"Goodnight, Lizbett, as I will be with you."

He kissed her warmly, then she watched him as he disappeared into his bed chamber, and stood almost sadly as she heard the click of the lock.

The house was quiet, and walking to his study she moved around the ornate desk given to him by the Prince, and sat down in the large animal hide chair.

Finding a paper and writing implement she began to make the list, crossing out names as she wrote them, finally ending with only three; Father, Mother, Tholl. She felt a lump in her throat. She had no friends. There were plenty of women who tittered around her but she could see right through them; they were only with her because she was the Princess and they wanted to bask in the glory of her position and power.

I suppose I haven't been much fun to be around. I was always angry about something, or with someone. That's all going to change now, I can feel it.

Folding the paper in half she placed in the top drawer, then had a thought, and pulling out a fresh sheet she started a note.

Dear Falayla:

Without your courage my wedding to Lord Larian Lobergene would not be taking place. You are just a young village maiden. What it must have taken for you to go against the will of someone as powerful as the Head Of The Court. How can such a debt be repaid?

I would be honored and humbled if you would agree to be my attendant at the wedding. If you

accept you will be brought here by a castle carriage, and be accommodated at Lord Lobergene's house.
I await your response.

Most sincerely,
Princess Lizbett Of Verdana

Feeling immensely satisfied with her letter she folded it and placed it in the drawer next to the list for Larian to find in the morning, then feeling unexpectedly tired she made her way to her bed chamber.

She changed into her nightdress, thinking how pleasant it was not to have her simpering servant fussing around, and slipping between the coverlets she closed her eyes with the image of Larian asleep in his bed just down the hall. It was comforting, but still she missed him, she missed him dearly.

When she arrived at the dining hall the following morning the house was already busy. The table was laden with food, and from the windows she could see the gardeners were working hard. The housekeeper informed her Larian was in his study and had been awaiting her arrival to join her.

"I will tell him you're here," she said formally, then curtsied and hurried away; a moment later, when he appeared, her heart leapt and her flippity flip jumped in her stomach.

"It is so good to see you," she beamed.

"Good morning, Princess," he smiled kissing her on her brow.

"Good morning, my Lord, or should I say, good morning, Commander, or good morning Warrior Of The First Order?"

"You're feeling cheeky this morning."

"No more than usual, well, perhaps a little, and I'm definitely feeling hungry…in more ways than one," she added with a wink and a whisper.

"I see," he grinned. "As to your question, good morning great one on high who spanks with a very hot hand, would be acceptable."

She laughed out loud and playfully punched him, then sitting down they began to eat, and he praised her note.

"It has already been sent out, and thank you for not inviting the many noble women I'm sure you know."

"I am not true friends with any of them, which makes me sad," she said honestly. "I hope that will change."

"As we grow in our life together you will attract those who genuinely like you," he said warmly. "Now I have something to discuss with you, but we must keep our voices low."

"That sounds intriguing," she remarked.

"First though, I have news. I have already received several messages from my Prince. He has assigned a team to prepare the house for the wedding. They will be here every day, beginning when the East sun rises, and staying until it begins to set. This includes a full kitchen staff who will be preparing the banquet."

"My goodness. Can your kitchen handle such a big chore?"

"They will make the necessary adjustments, and I suspect much of the food will start arriving from the Palace a few days before, but there are other things that need to be organized. The tables, for instance, are to be set out on the terrace, the settings and how the table is to be decorated must be decided."

"That's wonderful," she exclaimed. "I was going to suggest having the banquet there."

"There are also dressmakers that will be calling on you. I am embarrassed that I didn't have the foresight to see this eventuality and allow you to bring more clothing," he admitted, "but the court's tailors will be here to measure you and bring various materials so you may pick those you like. I have also asked your father to arrange to have some of your clothes sent here."

"You have thought of everything."

"I have tried to," he smiled. "The Palace of Zanderone isn't far, so that makes much of this easier than you might think. Oh, and the Prince is inviting your father and mother to be his guests there."

"That occurred to me as I fell asleep last night," she remarked. "It's the obvious solution. Will your uncle be performing your half of the ceremony?"

It was the custom in both Zanderone and Verdana that the father of both the bride and groom perform the ceremony, each for their child.

"This is more difficult," Larian sighed. "The Prince has stated he wishes to perform the task, but since he is not my closest male relative it may not be possible. Of course my uncle wishes it too, but he would never go against the Prince. If the law allows it, the Prince will do the honors, otherwise, yes, my uncle."

"What is it that we must talk about in quiet," she frowned.

"I was getting there" he said softly, "you must learn to be patient. With all the workers coming I fear our privacy will be compromised."

"Oh, I hadn't thought about that."

"It will be impossible to have safe time alone here in the house, and it's imperative that I continue to prepare you for our wedding night."

"And it's imperative that I have your attention," she whispered with her eyes wide. "I cannot live without it...I missed you so much through the night."

"There is a small cottage a short ride from here, and each morning, as the East sun rises, I will collect you from your room and take you there. It cannot be seen from the house and it's very comfortable. I plan on enlarging it and using it for staff when I need to, but for now it sits empty."

"Larian, that's wonderful," she beamed, "but what horse will I ride?"

"You'll be on Thunder with me. There are steps near the stable that you can use to climb on, and I've already put something in place at the cottage."

"Can we go there today?"

"I have planned on it," he whispered, "directly after we finish this meal. I will tell everyone that I am taking you around the grounds, which is something that must be done anyway, so you can see the fence that separates the property from the outside."

"I need to feel you," she said longingly, "I need your arms, your lips-"

"Hush, the housekeeper is coming."

She'd been leaning forward, and had settled back in her chair just moments before the woman walked in carrying a steaming pot of honey tea.

A short time later, thrilled with the pending arrangements and eager to see their cottage, Lizbett was very happy as she climbed up the steps outside the stable, and with Larian's help she found her spot on Thunder's wide back.

"I'm falling in love with him," she smiled as they began to walk away from the house.

"I think, with all the activity here, we should let Scarlet settle in until after the wedding. I saw her spooking at the gardner's barrow this morning."

"She is very nervous," Lizbett agreed, "but she is much easier to ride than you think."

"If you wish we can try, but I don't want anything happening to you, and she needs some proper training. She is your horse though, so..."

"I would love you to help me with her," Lizbett said quickly, "but perhaps you're right, perhaps I should wait until everything has calmed down, but I am going to visit her every day. I don't want her to think she's been abandoned."

"You must, this is important. Horses are very sensitive creatures."

"Larian your land is so lovely," she remarked as they made their way across the fields. "Are you going to bring in more animals?"

"Definitely, and I'd like you to help me decide what to have here."

The cottage came into view, and when they stopped, though she was still slightly nervous, she sat on Thunder while Larian slipped off, then slid down into his arms.

"Where can you tether him?" she asked, patting the horse's wide, thick neck.

"He won't go anywhere," Larian laughed, and opening the door he ushered her in.

"It's so inviting, it's like a little hideaway," she sighed.

"It is a little hideaway," he murmured as he took her into his arms. "Our little hideaway," and lifting her up he carried her through a narrow arch into the bed chamber and laid her on the mattress. "I came here early, made sure everything was clean and ready for us."

Quickly stripping, he began to slowly remove her dress and petticoats, then slipped down her silky underwear.

"I think I want you to go without these," he murmured as he put them aside.

"No! That would be…"

"That would be scandalous," he grinned, "but only you and I would know, and I like the idea of you running around the house without them under your many clothes. I could pull you into a corner and touch you any time I want."

"Oh, Larian, the things you say, the way you make me feel."

"I have something, a tool that I must use to help prepare you," he said tenderly as his hand roamed across her nakedness, "it will follow after I have used my finger for a while."

"Will it hurt?"

"No, not at all, it will feel very pleasant and bring you to a wonderful moment."

"I want to feel it now," she pleaded shifting on to her side and pressing her breasts against him.

"Such a passionate soul," he mumbled, and lowering his lips to her nipples he began to gently suck.

"Mmm, that is marvelous," she moaned raising her chest to meet his mouth.

Slipping his fingers between her legs he found her already wet and in need, and placing his hand on her waist he gently rolled her on to her stomach.

"As you were yesterday," he said slipping his arm down the side of the bed, "I just wish we had more time, I wish we could stay here until the East sun sets."

"Some time is better than none," she said softly as she lifted her hips and dropped to her elbows.

Holding the artificial phallus he'd hidden away he knelt behind her and gazed at her glistening sex.

"So beautiful," he muttered as he began to tease her with his fingers, "so beautiful and so hungry, alway so hungry."

She wriggled her response, making him break into a grin.

"I see you have no longer have concerns about this position."

"None," she replied, "just the opposite. It makes me feel even hungrier."

Sliding his large finger into her channel he began to move it in and out, and she responded immediately, opening and thrusting back.

"You may use your own hand against your precious nugget," he said softly.

Letting out a cry of gratitude she moved her fingers against her pulsing pussy, and with a mushrooming lust he watched her arousal grow; quickly able to add a second finger to the first he pumped her carefully with a consistent rhythm.

"I'm going to use the tool now," he warned, "it is smaller than my cock but larger than my two fingers together. All you have to do is relax and accept it," he purred, "and keep your fingers busy."

Made of a rubbery wood, it was hard but with a forgiving malleability, and as he pushed it forward she arched her back and spread her legs, eager to meet it.

"Oh, it is heaven," she moaned as he slithered it into her. "Please, Larian, please use it."

The gentle plunging began, and gripping his cock he stroked himself as he pumped, her wriggling behind and heavy sighs feeding his fire, rapidly bringing his cock to the edge. Had he more time he would have paused, but he knew they had to return before the sun rose too high.

"How are you?" he asked.

"Sir...I am...I am, oh, Sir, I love that thing inside me...and I am there!"

Determined to milk her properly he held himself at bay, and as she cried out her passionate bliss he continued to work her cunt, thrusting the phallus with quick strong strokes.

Her joyous wails began to transform into whimpers, and as her spasms receded, the last one being a heavy sigh, he let her collapse then rolled her on to her back. Gazing at her breasts he fervently massaged himself, and with a guttural groan he spewed his cream across her puckered nipples. The tingling prickles rippled through him, and panting heavily he dropped next to her, reaching under the pillow to retrieve a cloth.

"How did you know that was there?" she murmured as he softly wiped away the result of his climax.

"I put it there when I came earlier."

"You are so clever. I love our little hideaway, I love everything, especially you. Please can you hold me?"

"Of course," he whispered.

As he slid alongside her she nestled against him, and listened to the strong steady rhythm of his heart.

"Tomorrow morning," he said softly, "will be different."

"Different how?"

"Tomorrow I must begin your morning spankings. I will warm your bottom first, then I will pleasure you."

"Yes, Sir."

"Discipline will never be forgotten," he said firmly, and dropping his lips to hers he kissed her languidly, gently devouring her mouth, then traveling his kiss to her ear he added, "because we both know the Petulant Princess is never far away."

CHAPTER TWENTY-EIGHT

As she knew he would Larian kept his promise, and the following morning she found herself over his lap, squirming as his hand smacked the sensitive area where her thighs kissed her bottom. The spanking was rapid and sharp, and though quickly over it left her gasping and urgently wishing she could rub away the sting.

"Remember, there will be many people here every day until our wedding. They will be busy and probably nervous, wanting everything to be perfect," he said as his hand roamed over her cheeks. "You must be patient and kind. They will have questions, and if you're unsure you must find me."

"Yes, Sir," she whimpered, "I'll be good."

"I'll hear about it if you're not," he warned, "and I won't hesitate to add any naughtiness to my list."

"Ooh, that dreaded list," she groaned.

He toyed with her breasts more than he had before, keeping her on her back with her arms raised above her head, and exerted complete control over her body, but again time was their foe and he was forced to bring them to their end before he would have liked.

Their passionate secret mornings continued but he varied their play, and though it always began with a spanking he varied that as well, sometimes swatting the center of her full, round cheeks, other times bending her over pillows on the bed and landing his belt with a couple of lashes, whatever happened to take his fancy.

As the days slipped away he was able to replace the first artificial phallus with a second, larger one, and was confident that by the time their wedding night was upon them, he would have prepared her sufficiently to accept his large member.

Lizbett had made it a habit to visit Scarlet directly after lunch. Taking carrots, apples and melon from the table, she would carry them in a basket to the paddock where Scarlet was living. There were horses on either side, and Lizbett noticed her mare had begun making friends, and had taken a special liking for two gray geldings who looked like identical twins. They were older and very calm, and Lizbett guessed Scarlet was drawn to their mellow nature.

She would feed her the treats from the basket, but would scold her if she became to grabby, and to Lizbett's amazement Scarlet began to wait until the food was offered. Each time Scarlet was soft and easy, Lizbett would stroke her neck and talk to her softly, but if Scarlet was aggressive and tried to snatch the food from her hand or the basket, Lizbett made it very clear it was unacceptable.

"I'm so proud of her," Lizbett said to Larian over dinner one night. "She's being so good, and it didn't take much."

Larian smiled and nodded knowingly, delighted that Lizbett was finding a new and better path with her beloved mare.

One morning, however, there was no phallus, no warm caresses, and no pleasure for Lizbett; it was time to address the list. Entering the cottage he immediately ordered her to kneel in the center of the small living room.

"I don't know if you've been counting the passes of the moon, Lizbett, but it has come time to discuss your naughty list."

"The list? Oh, no."

"Yes, let me see here," he said sternly as he pulled a chair from the modest table and sat in front of her. "My goodness, you were a bad girl, but you've been quite well behaved since I began spanking you every morning."

He read of her list of naughty crimes, then announced how she would be disciplined for each one.

The first punishment she anticipated; he was going to rub her nugget until she was about to have her moment, then deny her.

The second she did not expect; following the time she spent with Scarlet after lunch, she had to return to her chamber and was not allowed out until the rise of the East sun the following morning, when he arrived to collect her.

"I will be sure your evening meal will be brought to you on a tray, but otherwise you will not be disturbed. I will tell everyone you are suffering from a pain in your head. The time alone will give you an opportunity to think about what a naughty girl you've been."

The third she found very unpleasant; when she was exiled to her chamber he was going to give her his dirty riding boots, a cloth and some polish, and she was to make them shine; it was the work of a servant girl.

"You have been much too proud and arrogant, and you must have a lesson in humility," he decreed.

Having laid sentence, he made her stand in front of him with her petticoats raised and her feet apart while he massaged her to the point of release, but then he had an additional surprise.

"I know how temptation can be," he said firmly, "so I have something to prevent you from making a grave error."

Opening a drawer on the sideboard he retrieved a long, thick piece of wadding with thin cord running through and around it. Where the wadding ended the cord continued, creating a tail on each end.

After tying a separate cord around her waist, he placed the center of the wadding between her legs, then pulled both tails of the cord tightly upward, sending the back one between her cheeks, then with an extra tug, tied both front and back tails to the cord he'd secured around her waist.

"You will not be able to undo those knots, Lizbett, nor will you be able to wriggle your fingers inside the wadding."

"Uh, Sir?" she mumbled, a red flush of embarrassment crossing her face, "what if I need to…uh…relieve myself."

"I will be checking on you, and will remove it when necessary," he said casually.

Any additional spanking was notably absent, and when they left the cottage, her tiny nugget throbbing with need and the wadding only adding to the hunger, she felt the weight of the discipline. Spanking would have been much easier to bear; her punishments carried far more unpleasantness.

The following morning, however, when the discipline was over, he was exceptionally affectionate and loving, and brought her to a spectacular climax.

"I promise I will try so very hard to please you," she whispered laying in his arms. "Those punishments were awful but that's not why. I will try hard because I want you to be proud of me."

"I am proud of you, but I am even prouder when you behave properly," he purred.

Falayla arrived later that day, and was thrilled by the honor. A cot had been placed in a small room off the kitchen, and though it was a tiny space the village maiden had never known a room of her own and was overjoyed. As the time passed, Lizbett gave her various tasks and found the girl not only to be bright and efficient but very easy to be around, and began considering her as her permanent personal servant.

On the last pass of the moons before their wedding the house finally began to look as the designers from the Palace had described. To compliment the color of the home they had chosen yellow and white flowers to grace the terrace, and when the tables had arrived and been put in place, Lizbett could envision how fabulous the banquet would be.

On the back lawn, where it had been decided the ceremony would take place, a white arch covered in pink and yellow blossoms was waiting, with three rows of chairs placed directly in front where the guests would be seated.

"It's all so exciting," she gushed standing on the lawn gazing at it.

"I heard you decided to have a new dress made," Larian whispered.

"Who told you?" she demanded. "It was supposed to be a surprise."

"It will be. I haven't seen it," he laughed.

That night they were obligated to attend a special dinner at the Prince's Palace in Zanderone. It was to be a small affair, with some nobles with whom Larian was acquainted and mutual friends of the King and the Prince.

Larian could not have been prouder of his bride. She glided through the night with grace and charm, was pleasant to everyone, and he heard many comments about her easy manner, and the soft mauve eyes that sparkled like the pinpricks in the sky. Traveling back to his house in the carriage he held her fondly on his lap, kissed her lips, then carried them to her neck to whisper in her ear.

"This time tomorrow we will be husband and wife," he purred, "and will be sleeping together through the full passes of the moon."

"I can't wait," she sighed resting her head against his shoulder, "and I can't wait to feel you...your cock...entering me." Her words sent his manhood surging to life, and sitting on his lap she felt it too. "It seems the feeling is mutual," she giggled.

"You have no idea, Princess," he sighed. "You know I won't be knocking on your door when the East sun rises."

"We didn't talk about it, but I assumed not."

"After breakfast I will not meet you again until we stand before your father and my uncle."

"Was the Prince very disappointed?"

"Yes, but tonight it was decided he would be with them during the ceremony, and though he can't do any of the speaking he is still appeased."

"My heart is beating so hard," she breathed. "I believe my eyes will not close at all tonight."

"I must enter Zinyana, otherwise mine will be staring out at the sky, and I want to be at full power for our wedding night."

"Oh, must you say such things?" she moaned.

The carriage rolled to the front of the house, and though the moons were high in the sky they found people still working on the decorations, and walking inside they could hear noise from the kitchen.

"It appears you will not be the only one who might lose sleep," Larian remarked.

"Falayla said she has a sleeping tonic, do you think I should take it?" she asked as they made their way up the stairs.

"I wouldn't. It might upset your stomach, and I'd rather you be a bit sleepy than sick."

"Very true," she nodded.

They reached her bed chamber, and taking her in his arms he held her tightly, then clutching her hair he gently tilted back her head.

"Listen to me," he said gently, his aqua eyes gazing into hers. "Tomorrow when we join our lives, when we say those special words, I will mean every one of them. I have loved you since we were silly and young, and that has taken on a strength and power that has stunned me. I will move mountains to protect you, Lizbett, and you will always come first."

"Larian," she breathed, the threat of tears making her throat hot, "I cannot move mountains as you can, but it is true, the power of my love feels as strong as you say."

His mouth found hers, and he kissed her with an urgent, demanding, prolonged kiss, a kiss that made her heart pound in her chest and her pussy pulse, and a kiss that shattered all other kisses they had ever shared.

"Tomorrow," he whispered as he broke away.

"Tomorrow," she repeated breathlessly.

He opened her door, watched her enter, then turning on his heel he strode away.

CHAPTER TWENTY-NINE

Standing under the arch, the yellow and pink flowers trailing around them, Larian thought Lizbett looked like a Goddess. Her long red hair was woven with sparkling thread, and her dress was yards upon yards of diaphanous folds of white and gold that floated around her like a cloud.

Dressed in his Commander's uniform, the vest of the Warrior Of The First Order glistening in the sun, the crisp cream shirt unable to hide his muscled arms, Lizbett felt weak as she gazed at him. He was taller and straighter than she'd ever seen him, and his aqua eyes were shining with the brightness of the East sun.

Her father was standing in front of her, his uncle in front of him, and between them the Prince just a few steps behind; the gathered guests fell silent as the King stepped forward.

"Princess Lizbett of Verdana, as your father I give you to this man, Lord Larian Lobergene. Is this your wish?"

"It is, father.

"Place one hand on your heart, and one hand on his."

Lizbett turned to face Larian, and as their eyes touched she felt a thick, warm stirring in her soul.

I have lived my whole life just to reach this moment. Larian, my stable boy, my warrior, my hero, my heart is going to burst.

"Place one hand on your heart, and one hand on his," the King repeated.

Breaking from the spell she raised her hands; resting her palm on her chest she could feel her heart beating, and when she slipped her other hand under his vest, it was as though their hearts were beating as one.

"Do you promise to nurse your beloved when he is sick, warm him when he is cold, cheer him when he is sad, miss him you are separated, lay only with him, and keep him in your heart before all others?"

"I do, father."

"Do you feel his heart beat with yours?"

"I do, father."

"Drop your arms to your sides."

The King stepped back, and Larian's uncle stepped forward.

"Lord Larian Lobergene, as your uncle, I give you to this woman, Princess Lizbett of Verdana. Is this your wish?"

"It is, Uncle.

"Place one hand on your heart, and one hand on hers."

Larian lifted his hands and gently placed one on her chest, and the other on his, and just as Lizbett had moments before, Larian felt the same flood of warmth wash over him.

"Do you promise to nurse your beloved when she is sick, warm her when she is cold, cheer her when she is sad, miss her when you are separated, lay only with her, and keep her in your heart before all others?"

"I do, Uncle."

"Do you feel her heart beat with yours?"

"I do, Uncle."

"Drop your arms to your sides."

Larian's uncle stepped back, and the King stepped forward and addressed the guests.

"The union of these two souls is forever. They make these promises in front of you, their dearest friends and loving family, to show their love and seek your blessing. Do you give your blessing?"

In unison the seated guests replied,

"We give our blessing."

Larian's uncle stepped forward.

"Is there anyone here who does not give their blessing?" he called.

He waited a beat then turned back to Larian.

"Larian, place your hand on her heart."

The King turned to Lizbett.

"Lizbett, place your hand on his heart, and the two of you speaking as one repeat this; I give my heart to you, it belongs only to you, and my love will cherish you through all our days together."

Fighting her joyful tears Lizbett began to speak first, then Larian joined in, finding his voice difficult to control, and when they'd finished the King told them to drop their hands.

"Larian, do you have a gift for your wife?" the King asked.

"I do," he smiled.

Turning to his uncle he accepted a black, square box and slowly lifted the lid, and as Lizbett gazed down she caught her breath; it was the most beautiful thing she had ever seen. A glittering mauve stone was set in gold, surrounded by smaller stones that sparkled like the sun twinkling on the waters of a lake, and a thick gold chain was threaded through a ring at the top.

"I give you this gift as a token of my love," Larian began. "The stone is like your infinite mauve eyes as they gaze at me, your pure soul shining through them. The sparkling stones that surround it are like the pinpricks in the night sky that live in infinity, as does our love. This will hover next to your heart so you will feel my love as I feel yours, so you may raise your hand and touch it, as you touch my soul. The gold is precious, as you are precious, and the stones can never be ground or broken. Like us they will endure forever."

Lifting the pendant from the box he placed it around her neck, and though his fingers were thick they were nimble, and he had the clasp quickly closed.

There was a murmuring through the guests, as was allowed, then Larian's uncle stepped forward.

"Lizbett, do you have a gift for your husband?"

"I do," she smiled, and took a silver metal box from her father.

Turning back to Larian she lifted the lid, and sitting in a swath of shining red fabric sat a wide wristband of silver woven with gold, clearly the work of an elite craftsman. It appeared to be thick and heavy, and in the center set in ebony, was the carving of a black horse with a flowing mane, four white socks and a white blaze over its face.

As Larian stared he felt an impossible lump in his throat; what she had done was perfection.

"I give you this gift as a token of my love," she managed as the tears began to flow. "It is strong, like you, it is precious, like you, it will grace your wrist so when you must fight, you will feel my love protecting you and giving your arm even greater strength. It shines, as your eyes shine at me with your soul's love. The black horse is Thunder, but it is also the thunder that you bring forth as a warrior, as a commander, and as a man. This band can never be dissolved, broken or set aflame and is, as we are, forever."

Handing the box to her father she lifted out the band, and as Larian offered his arm, she turned it sideways and slipped it over the narrow side of his wrist. Taking his other hand Larian squeezed it, closing it so it could not slip off.

The King stepped between them, and in a loud voice that was reserved for proclamations he began to speak.

"The vows have been made, the gifts have been offered and accepted, and by law I now declare, with much pride and joy, that Princess Lizbett of Verdana, and Lord Larian Lobergen of Zanderone, are wed."

The gathered crowd were silent, waiting to see how Larian would celebrate the moment and they were not disappointed. He placed his wide hands around her waist, kissed her lightly, then lifted her off her feet and spun her around. She squealed in delight and everyone was on their feet, clapping and cheering.

"We did it," she laughed as the tears spilled down her face. "We actually did it."

"Yes we did," he laughed back, as he placed her on her feet he whispered, "and you know you're in for a lifetime of spankings."

Looking up at him with twinkling eyes she whispered back, "I hope so."

CHAPTER THIRTY

Dances were danced, music was played, songs were sung, speeches were delivered, a feast was eaten, and much wine was consumed. The festivities continued until the moons began to descend in the sky, giving way to the East sun's light. There were moments during which someone would ask were Larian was, or searched for Lizbett, but with so much frivolity the question was soon forgotten and the hunt given up. It never occurred to anyone that the happy couple had eaten very little and drunk even less, and with Zoltaire's help they had climbed upon Thunder who had spirited them away to their cottage.

While Larian waited in the small living room, where just a few days before she'd been made to kneel and listen to her list of naughty crimes, Lizbett changed into her wedding night gown.

It was soft mauve, like her eyes, with strips of white lace sewn in a haphazard way, and rather than long and flowing as was the custom, she'd had the dressmaker cut it short, so it fell only to mid-thigh.

The dressmaker had tittered and scolded, but Lizbett would not be swayed and ignoring the disapproving words had ordered the woman to finish the garment, adding glittering stones around the low scooped neckline.

When the dressmaker asked about the petticoats, how many and what fabric, Lizbett had stunned the woman even more by stating there would be none, and nor did she didn't need any fine silk underwear.

The look on the dressmaker's face was so shocked Lizbett decided to spare the poor woman and told her she already had the perfect pair of underwear, and some very fine petticoats that had been sent from the castle.

Standing in the small bedroom she stared at herself in the reflecting glass. The nightdress was scandalous, and with nothing underneath it was doubly scandalous; it showed all her curves and the full extent of her legs, but her favorite part was how her nipples were pointing through the thin, flimsy fabric.

Larian had placed clean bedclothes on the mattress and brought two oil lamps from the house, one for the living area and one for the bedroom. With the night at its darkest with the waning moons, the single lamp was the only light, and it's soft luminescence gave her skin an incandescent glow, her mauve eyes depth, made the stones around the neck of her nightgown glitter, and gave the necklace around her neck a brilliant radiance.

"I'm ready," she called.

Larian had removed all his clothes except his vest, wanting to wear the significant garment for the first coupling with his bride. If there was ever a time to wear a garment that could be used only for special occasions, then this night would forever be at the top of that list.

Moving through the arched entry he stopped and stared, first at the pendant around her neck. Its sparkling intensity was mesmerizing, but when his eye dropped to the tiny twinkling beads around her neck that highlighted the top of her breasts, and continued down the wicked attire that stopped at mid-thigh, his cock, already at half-mast, sprang to life.

"There are no words," he mumbled. "What you are wearing? You must wear this every single day. How did you find such a garment?"

"I had it made," she boasted. "The dressmaker was horrified."

"I'm sure," he grinned, "but I am not. I am overcome."

Striding forward ran his fingers across her nipples pointing so unashamedly through the flimsy fabric.

"You are naked under this thing!" he exclaimed.

"I am, Sir," she giggled.

"Oh, Lizbett, you must be spanked for such wickedness," he declared, and moving to the bed he sat on the edge and laid her over his knee. "I shall spank you through this thin garment, then on your bare bottom."

"Of course you will," she said looking over her shoulder at him with a cheeky grin.

"What is that supposed to mean?"

"There was more than one reason I had it made," she giggled.

"Ooh you are so naughty," he said with mock sternness. "So you want to be spanked, do you? Well, then, spanked you shall be."

He smacked his hand with a decisive swat in the center of her bottom, his wide hand covering both cheeks.

"OW!"

"Yes, protest, you will protest some more," he declared smacking her again.

"OW!"

"And some more," he repeated landing another.

Pushing the slip of material up her back he smiled at the pink stain on her beautiful bottom.

"Not red enough."

"I don't know, I can't see it," she giggled. "I think you should let me up so I can see it in the reflecting glass."

"Such impudence!" he exclaimed pretending to be shocked. "You need to be profoundly spanked!"

Setting to work in an easy rhythm he slapped her with just enough force to bring a hot tingle to her skin, then touching between her legs he felt her warm dew and pressed his fingers into her trough.

"Oh, my sweet maiden," he purred, "are you ready for my powerful cock?"

"So ready, Larian, I've been ready for so long. I feel as if I've been ready since we were together all that time ago in the stables."

"I feel that way too," he said softly. "First though, I must adore your beautiful breasts. Lay on the bed."

As she crawled off his lap he couldn't resist giving her a final swat, and when she rolled on to her back, and her mauve eyes twinkled up at him, he shook his head.

"No woman should be so beguiling," he breathed.

Lowering himself on top of her he brought his hands to her breasts, and gripping them tightly through the fragile fabric he moved his mouth from one rosebud to the other.

His playful nipping and gentle sucking sent her moaning, and though she tried to lift her pelvis under him, his weight would not allow it. She could feel his rod, and the more attention he paid to her mounds the more she wanted to feel it slide inside her.

"Oh, Sir, that feels so amazing," she moaned, "but please, won't you take me?"

"Be assured I will definitely take you," he murmured, "but in my own time. The more you beg, the longer you will wait, unless your begging is so sincere it touches my heart."

"Larian, you are so hard," she groaned.

"Yes, I am, and yes, I am," he murmured lifting his head and winking at her.

She thumped his shoulder, but it only brought a painful nip to her red rosebuds in response.

"I surrender," she bleated, "do with me what you will."

"Ah, there you are," he smiled, "and while I think the words are only words said to achieve your end, I still like to hear them."

He rose up, and grabbing her hair he pressed his mouth upon hers, then did something new, something he'd been saving; he thrust his tongue between her teeth. She jolted, then began to relax as he explored her mouth; her tongue began responding, dancing with his.

"Larian," she gasped when he pulled back, "Larian, I must have you, please, it almost painful."

"This time I believe you," he crooned staring into her eyes, "but before I make you mine, I have another gift for you. It will surprise you, but you must sink into the feeling. I promise you will be very happy."

Swiftly moving down her body he lowered himself between her legs, and placing his hands on the insides of her thighs he pushed them apart.

"What are you doing?" she bleated staring down at him.

Scooting his palms under her warm cheeks he gripped them tightly, then placed his tongue on her sensitive nub. She wailed in shock, but ignoring her momentary panic he continued to swirl his tongue, pressing firmly, and covering her with his mouth he began to gently suck.

"Ooh, Sir, that is...that is...ooh..."

He lapped and kissed, nibbled and circled, then slid his finger forward, finding her culvert sopping and open. She cried out as his finger pumped and his tongue danced, then sitting up he clutched her hips and pulled her pelvis into his.

"Larian, that was magic, sheer, brilliant magic."

"This," he declared placing his swollen member at her entrance, "this is magic," and slowly pushing forward he made her his own.

Her pussy was beyond his imaginings, hot, tight, pulsing and needy, and she moaned her pleasure with every stroke.

"Tell me," he growled, "tell me how it feels."

"Like you are possessing me, it is so strong and big, there is no pain, just a demand for my surrender."

Her words drove him, compelling him to acutely fuck her, and pulling out he flipped her over, hauled her hips towards him, and surging forward began riding her with gusto. His moment was quickly upon him so he slowed, impaling her with soft, easy strokes, and raising his palm he caressed her pink backside before landing several hot swats.

"I am so close," she mewled, "but it's different. With every stroke of your mighty cock you bring me closer, but it's different, its deep, deep within me."

He was overjoyed. He had been taught women had two climatic moments; one was easy to achieve, and was accomplished by teasing her nugget, but the other was borne from thrusting, and while more difficult to attain it offered a greater, more profound pleasure.

"I shall ride you until you are there," he promised, and clenching his teeth he plunged forward.

He used all his discipline to stop himself from exploding, riding her then slowing, riding her even more forcefully, then slowing, but her moment seemed evasive; he was at the brink of thinking he had been too ambitious when suddenly, without warning, she began to wail.

Only once before had he heard the sound; it was deep, like a groundswell from the depths of her soul, and when her cavern walls clutched, grabbing him like a strong hand, he knew he had accomplished his goal and taken her to ecstasy.

The wailing continued as she gyrated her hips, and he held himself still, allowing her to do whatever she needed to savor the climax, but his cock would not be denied and began spewing inside her.

His eruption was all he'd hoped for, sparking his body with hot prickling tingles, and when her wails finally gave way to breathless gasps, his cock fell flaccid from her depths.

Collapsing next to her, believing his heart would soon leap from his chest if he didn't calm it, he could hear her softly sobbing.

"Lizbett," he cooed still trying to catch his breath, "did I hurt you? What's wrong?"

"I have no idea," she sniffled, "it just overwhelmed me and I felt so much."

He rocked her softly, feeling that she was softer and sweeter than before, that his uncle had been right. The power of his body uniting with hers was the key to their happiness, and her ultimate contentment.

"It has been an emotional day, and an even more emotional night," he said tenderly. "I vowed to hold you as you cry, or was it cheer you when you are sad?"

"I think it should be both," she replied smiling up at him between her tears. "I'm fine, it was an unexplained thing but it's passing. What I feel now is sheer happiness."

"To spend all night with you, every night, yes, sheer happiness," he murmured.

They drifted for a short time, then stirring to the feel of a chill she sat up and pulled the coverlets over them.

"Can I ask you something?" she said softly as she laid back down.

"Anything."

"That thing you did, when you put your tongue on me, that was…that was…"

"That was something very unique and will only happen on special occasions. I don't want to spoil you, you've been spoiled enough."

"What kind of occasions?" she pressed.

"Tonight obviously, as a special surprise and to show you there is always more I can give you, perhaps when we celebrate the changing of the seasons, or…" he paused, creating a dramatic moment…

"Or what?"

"Or, if you go for let's say, twenty passes of the moons, and there is nothing on your naughty list. If you can be that good I will give you that as a reward."

"That stupid naughty list," she grumbled.

"That stupid naughty list is about to be written upon if you keep complaining about it."

Flopping back down she mumbled,

"I can do that. I can go for twenty passes of the moon without doing something wrong, I'm sure I can."

"Princess," he purred, "you can do anything you want, have anything you want, you just have to want it badly enough."

"Like us," she sighed, "even after all that time, neither of us wanted anyone else, and here we are."

"And here we are."

EPILOGUE

Larian's uncle had arrived the morning of the wedding, and had been invited to stay as long as he wished. A warrior of warriors, with instincts and senses keener that even Larian's, he had seen the happy couple slip away long before anyone had noticed they'd disappeared, by which time nobody cared. He decided to wait three passes of the moons, and if they did not return he would leave. To his surprise they were home and at the midday meal the following day. Lizbett was aglow, and he'd never seen Larian more at peace.

When she excused herself, saying she needed a long soak, it left Larian and his uncle to have a talk. After discussing the ceremony and latest gossip, Larian took great pride in sharing the success of the naughty list.

"This is excellent," his uncle said proudly, "though I would advise not using it too long, it may loose some of its charm. You can always bring it back if you need to."

"If I do put it away for a time, what might you suggest in its place?"

"There is little a woman dislikes more than a solemn man around her, a man who is not happy with her but doesn't punish her. It sends a message that she has greatly displeased him."

"Ah, I can see that," Larian nodded.

"But this method can only be used sparingly, like the tongue on the nugget."

"Understood."

"When will you begin her training, in earnest I mean? Do you have a place ready?"

"She is a passionate soul, and responds fiercely. I believe it must be done slowly, and yes, I have a place. It is secret, and safe, and perfect."

"Excellent," his uncle nodded, "and now I think she is probably waiting for you to wash her back. This is the day after your wedding. It should not be intruded upon by an old relative."

"You're not old, and you could never intrude upon me. You could live here if you wished and we would be overjoyed to have you," Larian said warmly.

"I will be leaving as the West sun sets. I like to sleep in the carriage and wake up at home. It seems to make the journey shorter, and I like the rocking of the coach."

"We will be here to wave you off," Larian promised.

Standing up he grabbed a large slice of cake, and with a wink to his uncle he headed out of the room and up the stairs.

Entering his bed chamber he found the coverlets turned down, and placed the cake on a nearby table. Moving into the anteroom he found Lizbett laying back in the tub, her eyes closed, and petals of rosamine floating in the water.

"How did you get this filled so fast?" he asked as he walked over.

Opening her eyes she smiled up at him.

"Falayla. It was ready when I arrived," she answered sitting up. "She'd guessed I'd want a soak so she filled the tub after the morning meal. She is so thoughtful. May we keep her as my personal servant?"

"Yes, definitely," he nodded. "Why are the coverlets down?"

"Because after this soak I am going to take a nap. These last ten days have worn me out. I'm so weary...husband," she twinkled.

"I have brought you a piece of cake. It's on the table. You can have it just before you snooze."

"And what are you going to do? I know you won't want to sleep until much later."

"I have something I must attend to, then I'll be saying goodbye to Uncle."

"Will you come back and check on me when he leaves? If I'm awake I want to say goodbye."

"I will. Soak and sleep, my sweet wife," he smiled, then leaning down he softly kissed her.

Sinking back she watched him leave, and closing her eyes she let herself drift.

Marching to the stables, Larian had the stable boy saddle Thunder, then galloped him across the back fields of his property. It wasn't a long ride, but in the middle of the rolling hills it felt like the middle of nowhere, and slowing to a trot he approached the brick tower.

It wasn't a ruin, but a splendid well preserved fortress with solid wooden doors that opened to an expansive foyer. A large table sat in front of a fireplace, and he could well imagine warriors once seated there, sharing game cooked on a spit in the fire before them.

A nearby doorway led to a cozy chamber offering a large, carved, four poster bed. It sat proudly in the middle of the room, and had beckoned him the day he'd first walked in; when he'd brought fresh coverlets he was amazed at the lack of dust and dirt on those he pulled off.

Climbing the winding steps to another chamber that he'd initially found empty, he grinned as he opened the door and entered; during the days before he'd left to return to Verdana, he'd filled it with all manner of sexual devices. This was to be his training chamber, this was to be where Lizbett would learn about things she'd not even imagined, and he had a lifetime to teach her.

A while later, after spending time contemplating his days past and the days stretching ahead of him, he galloped Thunder home, returning in time to see his uncle into his carriage. Lizbett rose from his bed to be at his side, and as they waved goodbye he put his arm around her and hugged her tightly.

"Are you ready for what's ahead?" he asked.

Gazing into his aqua eyes she nodded her head.

"I am, whatever it may be. You were right, I am finding strength in not trying to be strong all the time. It's the oddest thing."

"The greatest freedom," he said solemnly, "can be found in giving up control."

* * * * * * * *

MAGGIE CARPENTER REVIEWS

I AM A DOMINANT
Review: G Jackson

"I am a Dominant" is the most honest telling of a Dominant's story that I have ever read. From the Author's bio and the Introduction I knew I was in for an ingenuous story. All you need to do is read the Kindle preview and you will be hooked. I understand the five-star streak of reviews because this beautifully written book consists of the most candid and fascinating portrayal of Dominance and Submission that I have come across. The writing itself is flawless, wonderfully edited. If you have never had any experience as a Dominant or Submissive, you will come away from reading this book with an entirely new perspective and all preconceived notions will be shattered. If you are experienced as a Dominant or Submissive you will be thrilled to find an author and subject so relatable and humanizing. James Collier is not the stereotypically fictionalized character with a dark past and tortured soul. The women whom he dominates are not witless, spineless, helpless creatures. Maggie Carpenter has captured the true essence of the Dominant/Submissive relationship and shared James Collier's story in a way that leaves a lasting impression. I cannot recommend this book highly enough to anyone (of appropriate age) with even the slightest interest in the non-vanilla. It is an extremely worthwhile, stimulating and fascinating read.

THE COWBOY'S RULES: 3: THE SURPRISE
Review: Lenell

I always enjoy reading about Cassie and Chad, they're like old friends and of course we can't forget Mickey. I love how she had Chad's horse showing in this book and Cassie's jumping. This book was HOT, hotter than the other ones I think, lots of sex and great spankings of course. Chad really helped bring out more of

Cassie's submissive side in this one. Also the finally get married in this one! which is bittersweet because it probably means this is the end of their adventure. It was a fun ride!

THE STRICT BRITISH BARRISTER
Review: CF
Just bought this a day or so ago, and I've already finished reading it. I buy books to escape into fantasy, and Ms. Carpenter never fails to fulfill that. This book is absolutely awesome. And I like the action right up front. Brittany and Duncan sizzle. (It's almost embarrassing what it does to me, too.) One of the best books by one of the best BDSM Romance authors out there. Well written. Thoughtful story. And it's hot. Loved it.

THE WANTED COWBOY
Review: Anonymous
What more could a book offer? Great read and I loved the plot. Luke and Tess are a fun couple and I want more of their story. I hope this is just the first book with them, and we can follow them as their relationship develops. This book has romance, intrigue, some truly entertaining secondary characters, and plenty of spanking and hot sex. Absolutely loved it, and will be reading it again (and again…).

THE HOURGLASS
Review: Laurel
Maggie Carpenter tops herself again. Every time I read one of her books, I think there's no way she can top this, but she does. This book has everything, romance, mysticism, coincidence, spanking and sensual sex and more. Beth had a crush on Michael for years but didn't have the nerve to talk to him. Michael fell in love with Beth but they never met. After the purchase of an hourglass, things begin to happen. Coincidence? Maybe, read and find out.

THE COWBOY'S RULES: 2

Review: Dimples

What an entertaining story. The people were great, the dog fantastic. Please write a continuing story. A very happy read. Loved every page.

THE COWBOY'S SECRET

Review: Love's Kitten

No one writes sex scenes like Maggie Carpenter! I've said it before and I will keep saying it so long as she keeps writing these smokin' hot page turners! You will be drawn in by the storyline that is fast paced and imaginative, and the sex scenes will make you weep with wanting. Trust me. A MUST read, perfect for the beach or a cold, rainy day!

A PROMISE OF PASSION

Reviewer: James

From the first word, I was spellbound by Maggie Carpenter's wonderful tale. Her wonderful story flows beautifully and you will fall in love with her characters, because they truly come to life and leap off the pages! This book has everything you could want in a story: romance, an exciting plot and a handsome, dominant hero who will capture your heart. This book not only promises passion, it delivers!! A must read!

THE COWBOY'S RULES

Reviewer: Jule Kijek

This was my first book by this author but it will NOT be my last. I liked that it was a full sized novel. Chad is a super hot cowboy looking to help out a friend. Cassie is a spoiled rich girl in desperate need of a spanking. Toss in horses, horse shows and a lovable dog named McTavish and you have a runaway hit. I just LOVED it. So worth the time and money!

THE ROCK STAR AND THE COWGIRL

Reviewer: JoJo Bear

I'm a Maggie Carpenter fan, and I snatched this one up as soon as I saw it. NO disappointments here. Don't want to give any spoilers, but a naughty "good" girl gets what she deserves and so does a very naughty bad girl. Plenty of hot sex, hot spankings and lots of romance.

THE BRITISH BILLIONAIRE BACHELOR

Reviewer: Desiree Holt

As one who usually reads and writes heavy BDSM books, I found Maggie Carpenter's treatment light and refreshing. Simon, thank heavens, is NOT your usual stuffy, it's-all-about-me billionaires, but a human with doubts and insecurities along with his self confidence. And Belle Somers, well, you just want to give her a hug. The story is entertaining but the strength is in the characters. The author makes them come alive for you and they stay with you long after you turn the last page. A fun read I recommend for anyone who wants to escape with a glass of wine and a good book.

THE BRITISH BILLIONAIRE BACHELOR - ACT II

Reviewer Paige Matthews

This is another wonderful read by Ms. Carpenter and I full believe readers will love Simon as much as I did. I am eagerly waiting for the third act of their story and anticipating Simon's revenge. :) Want to find out what I am talking about? Pick up this read and find out!

THE BRITISH BILLIONAIRE BACHELOR - ACT III

Reivew: Emily Tilton

I'm going to level with you. I read D/s erotic romance for the D/s sex. Ms. Carpenter puts a great deal of plot and character around her D/s sex, and that stuff is solid, but I need to be honest and say that that's not why I'm reading a book by Maggie Carpenter. I'm reading a book by Maggie Carpenter because she writes the transition from sweet romance to D/s better than almost anyone else I know. She doesn't disappoint here: Belle (sweet submissive) and her sister Lucinda (brat) both go on D/s journeys with Simon (cultured billionaire) and Joseph (rough and tumble chauffeur) that provide plenty of hotness—especially (for my own taste) when Simon begins Belle's training. If you like young women under tables servicing the men they call "Sir," you'll love this book.

THE SPANKING PSYCHIATRIST
Reviewer CF
Of all the dominant-submissive books I've read, this one is by far the most clever and the most captivating. The story is strong. It's not just words wrapped around spanking scenes. It's so believable, you can feel the emotions of the characters. And you'll never expect the ending! Dr. Montgomery is simply irresistible, too. If I could find his office, I'd make an appointment.

Visit the author at:
www.maggiecarpenter.com
www.MaggieCarpenter.com/blog
www.facebook.com/MaggieCarpenterWriter
www.twitter.com/magcarpenter2

PREVIOUS MAGGIE CARPENTER NOVELS

I Am A Dominant
The Cowboy's Rules: 3: The Surprise
The Strict British Barrister
The Wanted Cowboy
The Hourglass
The Cowboy's Rules: 2
The Cowboy's Secret
A Promise of Passion
The Cowboy From Down Under
The Romantic Dominant
The Cowboy's Rules
The Rock Star and The Cowgirl
The British Billionaire Bachelor
The British Billionaire Bachelor Act II
The British Billionaire Bachelor Act III
The Spanking Psychiatrist
The Billionaire's Daughter
Covert Cravings
Malibu Heat
Déjà Vu
An Eternal Flame - (*Déjà Vu–Book Two*)
Elizabeth's Education
The Inheritance - (*Elizabeth's Education–Book Two*)